The Honeymoon Prize

The Honeymoon Prize

An Ever After Romance

Melissa McClone

TULE
PUBLISHING

Chapter One

THE BREEZE OFF San Diego Bay ruffled the hem of Adelaide Sinclair's borrowed white dress. She stood at the wedding arbor in the County Administration Center's Waterfront Park, holding a single yellow rose, her pulse racing faster than an F/A-18 taking off from Miramar.

Don't lock your knees.

Passing out during the lunchtime ceremony would be a total wedding *faux pas*. Not what she needed when she already felt like a complete fraud, fake, liar. Her stomach churned, trying to wash away the guilt.

Clicks sounded—photographs being taken by her friend Emily Rodgers. The digital images weren't fun shots to be shared via Instagram, but pictures to place in a fancy white album, a remembrance of the wedding day.

Air rushed from Addie's lungs. *Breathe.* But less and less oxygen seemed to go into her lungs. Uh-oh.

Do. Not. Lose. It.

Nick Cahill, a close friend since kindergarten, stood next to her. The wind blew the ends of his wavy light brown hair,

1

making him look like a model. He wore black trousers, a slightly wrinkled white dress shirt and a black bowtie. He looked so handsome and groom-like. Well, of course he did, given he was the groom.

Her groom.

He'd been her best bud until middle school, an intermittent crush through high school and her platonic male BFF since then. She never thought she'd be adding *her groom* to the list.

Addie's forehead throbbed. Her heart ached. A lump burned in her throat.

I can't believe this is happening.

Once upon a time, like most little girls, she'd dreamed of marrying her own Prince Charming. She'd imagined a wedding ceremony on the beach at the Del—the Hotel del Coronado—within walking distance from her grandmother's house where Addie had grown up, hearing waves rolling to shore and seabirds overhead during the ceremony, feeling hot sand beneath her feet and surrounded by loved ones.

But dreams, like life, didn't always turn out as one planned. She hadn't finished college. She hadn't found true love. She hadn't been able to keep her grandmother alive any longer. The weight of the past four months pressed down on her shoulders and her eyes stung.

Instead of getting married on the beach, she stood in the city park by her friend Nick's side, listening to noise from the traffic on busy Harbor Drive and a siren somewhere off in the distance. Emily was their sole guest, spending her lunch hour being both a witness to the civil marriage ceremony and the wedding photographer. There wouldn't be a reception. No first dance, no tiered wedding cake, no bouquet toss, no champagne toast. The only pictures would be the ones Emily took with her new digital SLR camera.

Not that Addie had much of a choice.

With no money, no job and no place to live, Nick's plan to be married in-name-only for the next five years so he could keep his job, and she could get back on her feet sounded like a gift from heaven. But after exchanging vows and rings with a man who didn't know the meaning of the word commitment, the desire to be marrying her Prince Charming grew stronger by the second.

Stop. Addie should be . . . grateful. G-R-A-T-E-F-U-L.

Nick's suit of armor might be tarnished, but he was her white knight today, her hero, rescuing Addie like he was still a Special Forces soldier, only without his Green Beret. A good thing her heart knew not to fall for a heartbreaker like him. The women Nick dated were endangered species that vanished quickly. As his friend, she'd remained a part of his life much longer, twenty-two years and counting. One day, she would find her Mr. Right and marry for real. Until then she needed to . . . chill.

So what if she was putting her dreams of having a family on hold for another five years? That would make finding true love more special.

A smile tugged on her tight lips despite the chaos in her life and her swirling emotions. Thanks to Nick's generous offer, she would no longer have to sleep on Emily's couch or spend the day at the library using free computers to apply for jobs or search vending machines for spare change to fill her empty wallet.

His no-sex, married in-name-only proposal had saved her after being attacked by her family of vultures hell-bent on selling her late grandmother's Coronado cottage—a tiny, teardown perched on a million-dollar piece of property. A house promised to Addie after being Grammy's caregiver for the past nine years. Too bad promises weren't worth as much as a piece of Grammy's cottage pie.

Her grandmother's wishes had been ignored by Addie's aunt and mother, neither who visited over the years or contributed to Grammy's care or attended the funeral. Addie had consulted an estate lawyer about challenging the will, but the slim chance of winning wasn't worth the expense. Not fair, but then again, life wasn't.

"You may kiss the bride."

The Commissioner of Civil Marriage's words rattled around Addie's brain.

Kiss. The. Bride.

Addie's stomach plummeted to the tips of her sparkly silver knock-off Toms, her something *new* purchased for the wedding. How could she have forgotten the kissing part?

She balled her hands, wishing her one true love stood

next to her instead of her best bud. If only this ceremony involved two people exchanging meaningful vows with intent, not a sham with a divorce date decided upon.

Something sharp poked into her left palm. A thorn on the stem of the single yellow rose she held. Yellow—the color of friendship.

Nick was her friend. They'd never kissed beyond a peck on the cheek. Her girlfriends who'd dated him had told Addie that his kisses curled their toes. Her toes hadn't done anything but crack in years.

He cleared his throat.

"You may kiss the bride," the commissioner repeated, as if she hadn't heard him the first time.

But she had.

Anticipation and curiosity surged.

In Cancun after high school graduation, she'd thought he wanted to kiss her. She'd stood on hot sand on a beautiful beach in Mexico, the faint scent of a bottle of Corona on his warm breath, listening to him say he'd enlisted in the army and would be heading to basic training when they returned to San Diego. Oh, how she'd wanted to kiss him, but in typical Nick fashion, he'd backed away and pretended the moment never happened. She'd decided, then and there, to stop crushing and daydreaming about him. Nick would never be anything but her friend. Not even after they said "I do."

"Come on, Addie. It's no big deal," Nick whispered, as if

talking about grabbing hot wings and beer after a Padre's baseball game. "Let's get this over with."

Her gaze met his killer baby blues. She inhaled slowly, knowing he was right. Why was she hesitating? She would finally get that kiss she'd wanted. Well, sort of. The kiss like their marriage wouldn't be real. Addie lifted her chin.

Nick lowered his mouth. His lips touched the left half of her lips and part of her cheek.

For a nanosecond.

He drew back, his eyes darkening for a moment, before returning to their normal color.

Okay, that had been . . . nothing much. Disappointing. No toe curling. Not even a tingle.

Marriage in name only, Addie reminded herself. They'd agreed to a plan and set boundaries. Two friends cohabitating and sharing the benefits of marriage, except the emotional and physical bonds. Not having a reaction to the kiss was good, right? She rubbed the spot of blood away from where the thorn had poked her skin.

"I pronounce you husband and wife," the Commissioner announced with a relieved smile. "Congratulations. Let's pose for a quick picture. I have another appointment. I'll take your marriage license into the office so your wedding can be registered. Certified copies will be available in a week."

They turned so the wedding arbor was behind them. Nick struck a pose like this was a prom picture, not one from their wedding. Then again, these photographs had been Emily's idea. The album, too. Neither Addie nor Nick would ever thumb through the pages reminiscing about their wedding day.

"Smile." Emily snapped at least ten more pictures. "I'll put the best ones in the album so you can show your future children."

Addie's insides trembled. She hoped her outsides weren't shaking, too. Pretending in front of her friend was hard. She hated lying. "Thanks."

Emily adjusted the lens on her camera. "Let me take a picture of your wedding rings."

Addie placed her hand next to Nick's.

Emily's forehead creased. "Why aren't you wearing your grandmother's ring?"

Addie's heart panged. Her grandmother had given her the ring, a priceless, thoughtful birthday gift last year. "I sold the engagement ring to cover funeral expenses, remember?"

"Yes, but—"

"Addie wanted matching gold bands like her grandparents wore," Nick added. "Take the picture."

Emily did.

"I appreciate you being here, photographing the wedding and loaning me this beautiful dress," Addie said.

"Least I can do." Emily aimed the camera at them again. "Even when I dated Nick in high school, I had a feeling the two of you would get married someday. Everyone thought that."

"Why would you think we'd end up together?" The excitement in her friend's voice made Addie feel worse about the wedding charade. "Just because we were best friends didn't mean something romantic was going on."

He slid his arm around Addie's waist, his six-foot-tall frame casting a long shadow. He gave her a half-hug, something he'd done for as long as she remembered. "Why wouldn't we get married? If you remember, I proposed years ago."

"I haven't forgotten," Addie said. "But let me refresh your memory with two pertinent details. We were five and in kindergarten. I'm sure there's a statute of limitations on marriage proposals."

Emily laughed. "A man who knew what he wanted even back then."

To date as many girls as possible. Most of them her friends. Addie shook the thought from her head.

"I sure did," Nick said. "I always knew Addie and I were meant to be."

The words slipped so easily from his mouth she almost believed them, but this was nothing more than a performance. If Emily thought Nick and Addie were marrying for love, so would the rest of their friends. But all this made her wonder what she'd gotten herself into. Regret and guilt coated her mouth like a cough syrup. She swallowed, but knew the taste would linger a long time. "That's news to me because I remember your exact words back in kindergarten. You said we'd get married after we were old and fat and no one else wanted us. Not exactly the most romantic proposal."

Nor had she ever believed his words would come true.

Nick winked. "But memorable."

"Unforgettable." Addie looked up at him with a smile. He always made her feel better. "I'll give you credit for that."

Emily took another picture, then lowered the camera. "Seriously, you guys are the cutest couple."

Fake couple. Addie's smile faltered.

"Yes, we are." He pulled Addie closer. "Mr. and Mrs. Cahill, a.k.a. the cutest couple ever. We need matching T-shirts made for the honeymoon."

His playful tone should have brought back her smile. He knew Addie was keeping her name, but heat rushed up her neck anyway. "T-shirts aren't necessary. We each won a brand new vacation wardrobe along with the honeymoon."

Emily shimmied her shoulders. "You are going to have the most amazing trip."

"Thanks to you." Addie couldn't believe Emily's excitement. You'd think she was the bride. Then again, maybe she wanted her couch back and to be roommate-free. "I can't believe you entered us into a honeymoon contest, and we won an all-expenses-paid, ten-day-long, tropical getaway."

Anticipation for the trip, Addie's first vacation in years, had kept her going while dealing with her family and moving her few belongings into Nick's guest bedroom where she'd be living.

"My pleasure." Emily curtsied. "You will love Starfish Island. I saw the brochures. It's beautiful and romantic. Perfect for the two of you."

Maybe, except once Nick and Addie arrived on the private island resort in the South Pacific, beyond taking a few promo photographs and sharing a *bure*, the Fijian name for the thatched-roofed cottage, they planned to go their separate ways.

"Yeah, thanks." Nick dropped his hand from her shoulder. "I was going through the travel documents you gave me. A few pages seem to be missing."

"Really?" Emily fiddled with her camera strap. "I gave you everything I received from the travel company."

"Some sort of release was mentioned, but the information wasn't in the package."

"I'm sure you have everything." She dropped a lens cap, then swiped the piece of black plastic from the pavement. "I'll check when I get home from work and text if I find anything, okay?"

"Thanks," Nick said. "Seemed a little strange."

"I know my phone is in here somewhere." Emily dug through her bag. A package of tissue nearly fell out. She removed her mobile phone, glancing at the screen. "Would you look at the time? My lunch break is almost over. I need to get back to work. Pronto."

Addie touched her friend's shoulder. "Wait. Your dress."

"Keep it. Looks better on you, than me." Emily took two steps back. Her gaze traveled from Addie to Nick. "Have a great time in Fiji. Send me a postcard."

With that, Emily disappeared out of the park.

Addie looked at the empty spot where her friend had last stood. "She's in a hurry."

"Short lunch break," Nick said. "Might have a project due. Advertising is a high pressure business."

"Maybe." Emily dropping things and rummaging through her purse wasn't normal behavior for the ultra-organized, always-put-together ad executive. Nothing was out of place in Emily's apartment or life. Her spice rack and items in the refrigerator were alphabetized and put in order with expiration dates noted. "But she was acting . . . odd."

"Don't worry about Emily. She's always has everything under control." With his hand at the small of Addie's back, Nick led her to the street where his truck was parked at a metered spot on the curb. "Come on."

Typical Nick. Always in a hurry pushing her along when she'd rather hang back. He'd done the same thing during second grade recess every day to make sure they claimed the monkey bars before anyone else. She'd appreciated him bringing her along, and here they were again . . .

Some things never changed, even if their marital status had. Guess she should update her Facebook profile. *It's complicated* might be better than *married*, but that wouldn't be acceptable to Nick's boss, who was thrilled his most valuable employee was settling down. Kind of silly if you asked Addie. A wedding ring on Nick's finger might appease male clients, but a gold band would not make Nick any less attractive to said clients' wives. But if he kept his dream job and made his boss happy, who was Addie to bring up reality?

A bus dropped off passengers at the corner. A horn honked. Icky smelling exhaust from a passing cement truck made Addie crinkle her nose.

Nick glanced at the gold band on his left-hand ring finger. "I expected being married to feel different, but it's only been a couple of minutes."

She looked at her matching wedding band, shiny beneath the afternoon sun. The pleasant summer weather didn't match her mood at all. "I feel like a Miss, not a Mrs."

"Well, you've got five years to get used to the title."

Five years.

That suddenly seemed like a long time to play house. Dating while caring for her grandmother had been impossible. She'd tried a few times over the years. But given up. Still she believed in love, the forever kind that would last a lifetime. Someday she would find that. Someday . . .

He touched her arm. "Hey, what's wrong?"

"Nothing, just . . ." In spite of her doubts, Addie hoped Nick understood the depth of her gratitude. A week ago, she'd forgotten her key to Emily's apartment and fallen asleep on the welcome mat leaning against the front door, waiting for her friend to return from a date. "Thanks for everything. I owe you big time."

"Thank you." He flashed her a charming smile that sent female hearts aflutter, brought women to their knees at bars and clubs, and convinced Addie to accept his marriage-of-convenience proposal. Not that saying yes took much convincing. Desperation had a way of making a person see the brighter side to any option, including marrying her closest guy friend. "Without legal proof I was a one woman guy, my boss would ship me off to some boring assignment guarding a building or I'd be looking for a new job."

"I'd be homeless."

He winked. "You win."

"We both win and get a free honeymoon out of the deal." Though the rock in her stomach felt more like dread than relief at the moment.

"True that." He opened the truck's passenger door. "Here's to having fun and being each other's good luck charm from now on."

"I like the sound of that." She hoped his words came true. For years her luck had been bad. Not anyone's fault, just the way her life had turned out. She was ready for things to be different. "Where to now?"

"Home so we can finish packing our overnight bags."

Addie climbed up into her seat, careful with the dress. "I still can't believe we won a honeymoon. We'll have to buy Emily a nice souvenir."

Nick walked around the front of the truck and climbed

inside. "She's gone out of her way for us."

"That's because she thinks we're . . ." Addie couldn't say the words *in love*. "A cute couple."

"Yeah." He fastened his seatbelt. "But we can't tell her or anyone the truth. Our friends have to believe we're married for real. My boss, too. I love my job. Six figures to babysit clients in exotic locales is too easy a gig to lose because of a jealous husband."

The gorgeous, young wife of a client had become infatuated with her handsome bodyguard. The man threatened to take his private security needs elsewhere unless Nick was reassigned. With the man's connections, other clients voiced similar concerns leading to Nick's assignments becoming limited. His boss had joked how much easier life would be if Nick were married, but the underlying ultimatum was unmistakable.

So what did the not-interested-in-settling-down body-guard bachelor do? Propose to Addie. His friend. A sex-less, in name only marriage solved both their problems. In theory at least.

"Did you happen to give the client any reason to be jealous?" she asked.

"No way. I take my job seriously. No messing around. Strictly professional."

She had no reason not to believe him. Nick had never lied to her. But that meant she knew many of his secrets. "Until you're off duty."

He stuck his key in the ignition. "I'm only human, babe."

"I know." She was a one-man woman who wanted the happily ever after, pinning her heart on a guy like him would be a disaster. "And you can't help yourself for being a chick magnet."

His cheeks reddened. The charming blush reminded her of the boy he'd once been, the boy she'd once loved, her childhood friend. "A cross I must bear."

She fastened her seat belt, thinking about the cocktail waitress he'd last dated. They'd gone out for two weeks, a new record for him. "I pity any woman who falls in love with you."

He started the engine. "Funny words coming from the new Mrs. Cahill."

"In name only, dude. I would never want to be married to you for real." She knew too much about his dating habits. "No offense."

"None taken." He turned on his blinker. "I've never wanted to be married for real."

She remembered when he'd become engaged to a woman named Carrie who'd told him she was pregnant while he was deployed in Afghanistan. Nick, who wanted to do the right thing and be a better dad than his had been, proposed via Skype and sent her his paychecks, only to return home to find a pregnant fiancée, but one who wasn't far along enough for the baby to be his. She'd been lying and cheating on him the entire time.

Nick never mentioned Carrie, but Addie knew the breakup affected him. He'd left the military when his contract expired instead of reenlisting. His dates never went beyond casual, even back in high school, but they seemed to be more temporary and physical now. But the hookups seemed to satisfy him.

"At least we know where we stand," Addie said.

He nodded. "There's no one else I trust enough to marry like this. Things are going to be okay. This will work."

Addie crossed her fingers. She sure hoped so. Being homeless sucked.

Chapter Two

NICK STRETCHED OUT, enjoying the legroom in first class, thirty-seven thousand feet over the Pacific Ocean. He twisted the gold band on his left-hand ring finger.

Sunlight streamed through the plane's window, a new day. He hadn't been married twenty-four hours yet, but he'd realized one thing. This ring wasn't coming off his finger anytime soon.

Five years. He planned to make the most of being married.

Addie had called him a chick magnet, but this ring drew babes in like a tractor beam set on high. Since saying "I do," three hot women had tried giving him their numbers at the airport. He hadn't taken them. That wouldn't have been nice to do to Addie a few hours after their wedding, even if the marriage wasn't real. But getting married might be the best thing that ever happened to his social life.

With a wife waiting at home, *another* woman couldn't

expect him to get *serious* or stay the night. The possibilities of what he could get away with over the next five years were endless thanks to Mrs. Cahill.

Addie.

A warm feeling settled in the center of his chest, adding to the satisfaction he'd felt since being pronounced husband and wife. He'd come up with a brilliant plan.

This marriage wasn't only for him, but Addie, too. He would support her financially and pay her school tuition. She could enjoy life for once with no money or housing worries. He also had a special wedding present he'd tracked down for her, but he hadn't decided when to give her the gift. Maybe after they got settled on the island. He couldn't wait to surprise her.

Lying on her reclined seat, Addie slept, covered haphazardly with a blanket, her left calf sticking out and her feet covered in the fuzzy socks from their flight amenity kits.

She'd dressed for comfort, wearing cut-off knee-length sweats, a large t-shirt and oversized San Diego Chargers crewneck sweatshirt. She looked younger, like a teenager, with her dark brown hair pulled back in a familiar ponytail, the same style she'd worn for over two decades and freckles scattered across the bridge of her nose and cheeks.

Cute, as always, but different from how pretty she'd looked in the white dress at the wedding. The last time he'd seen her dressed up had been at prom. She'd gone with Scott Taylor, captain of the tennis team, and Nick had stewed watching the jerk hold Addie too close while they danced.

A bad night.

His fault.

He could have been Addie's prom date, her boyfriend even, except he'd blown her off on what would have been their first date. That day, his parents had finally, after years of threats and separating only to reunite, decided to divorce. Addie was his best female friend, his safety net. Going on a date had seemed like a bad idea. He'd been upset and too nervous to tell her how he felt, unsure of her feelings for him. He couldn't afford to lose her friendship. Not when his life was falling apart. He knew that might happen because he didn't know how to have a relationship that lasted more than a couple weeks or month.

Things had worked out for the best. Addie hadn't been pissed at him or wanted an apology, proving she must not have been into him enough to want to go out. They'd stayed friends, good friends, though they hadn't spent much time together after graduating because of his being away so much, and now they were married. At least according to San Diego County.

Goosebumps covered her arms. The air temperature in the cabin was cool at altitude. She'd mentioned not flying much. He turned off the air vent, then adjusted the blanket so she was fully covered.

She didn't stir. After what she'd been through the past months, she must be exhausted. She needed this vacation.

He pushed a strand of hair off her face, her skin smooth beneath the pad of his fingertip.

Ten days on the exclusive, private Starfish Island would get rid of those dark, puffy circles under Addie's hazel eyes. Relaxing would erase the two lines of worry forming a permanent V above the top of her nose. She could learn to have fun, be herself again, and not think about anyone but herself. Something she couldn't do caring for her grand-mother.

A flight attendant named Teresa touched the back of his seat. "Your wife looks like a painting. Very pretty."

Nick pulled his hand back, not realizing he was still touching Addie. "I'm a lucky man."

And he was. He couldn't ask for a better friend. Addie Sinclair was a total sweetheart with a generous heart. She'd cared for her ill grandmother, pushing her around in a wheelchair, driving her to one doctor appointment after another, for nine freaking years. Addie deserved a medal or something. Whenever he was deployed, she emailed him and sent a weekly care package. She was the only woman he'd ever trusted with his secrets, with everything.

But friendship was all they would have because nothing else lasted. His parents constant fighting and numerous affairs showed Nick marriage wasn't all hearts and roses. Carrie's lies and cheating had taught him emotions were best pushed aside and ignored. "Addie is one of a kind."

Teresa's smile softened. "Is there anything I can get for

you, Mr. Cahill?"

Not for him, but Nick wanted to make this trip special for Addie. He knew how to start—a toast to this new chapter in their twenty-two year friendship. "Two mimosas, please."

"Anything else?"

"Peanuts." Addie hadn't cared for the caviar, but she'd liked the little foil pouches containing peanuts.

"Mimosas and peanuts coming right up." The flight attendant walked to the front of the cabin.

As if on cue, Addie blinked open her eyes.

He looked away so she wouldn't catch him staring.

She stretched her arms over her head and yawned. "Are we there yet?"

"A couple more hours."

She glanced out the window. "It's daytime."

"It's also tomorrow. We crossed the dateline."

"Fiji is nineteen hours ahead of San Diego." She spoke softly, her tone hushed no doubt due to the other passengers in first class still sleeping.

"Someone's been using Google."

Addie shrugged. "Figured I should know a few things about where we're going. It's better if we stay awake now that it's daylight."

"Why?"

"So we'll be ready for bed five hours earlier than normal."

"You always have a plan." Addie had been making plans

for as long as he'd known her, from earning money at Coronado's Fourth of July parade, selling water bottles from her wagon to working as a waitress at a coffee shop on Orange Avenue to pay for college. Money she ended up spending on property taxes and other expenses for her grandmother's bungalow instead.

"Not really. I've given up planning. Seems like all mine fizzle out. Case in point, Grammy's will."

The resignation in Addie's voice bothered him. "Choosing not to challenge the will wasn't a fizzle. You made the best choice for yourself."

"And my bank account." She shook her head. "Who knew lawyers could be so expensive?"

"A lawsuit would have taken time and energy. You cut your losses and walked away. No shame there."

"I suppose."

He wanted her to have a positive outlook and be happy. The way she'd been when they were younger. "Times are changing for the better. No more worries. You have a place to live, food to eat, medical insurance, and tuition. I've ordered you credit cards and a debit card. Everything will be covered. I promise, it's going to be okay. You'll get your nursing degree the way you've talked about and find a great job at a hospital somewhere."

The edges of her mouth curved slightly. "You're such a good friend."

Nick would have preferred a grin, but he'd take a half-smile . . . for now. "Feeling's mutual."

Teresa returned with the mimosas in hand and her apron pocket full of peanut packages. "Your drinks and snacks."

Nick took the champagne flutes and handed one to Addie. Teresa placed the peanuts on the wide armrest then walked away. He raised his glass. "May our marriage be exactly what we want it to be."

Addie tapped her glass against his. The chime hung in the air above the monotonous drone of the engines. "I feel like a CD with a scratch, but thanks again."

A good thing he wore a seatbelt. Otherwise, the gratitude in her eyes would have knocked him to the floor. A funny feeling tickled his stomach. No one had ever looked at him like he was the sun in their world, but he was glad Addie did. He wanted her to be happy. "You're welcome."

They were doing their own thing on the island, but he hoped they could spend time together, share a meal or two, something they hadn't done much of since high school. "What's the first thing you want to do when we arrive?"

"Shower."

"After that."

She tilted her chin as if deep in thought. "A walk on the beach."

"You did that almost every day growing up in Coronado."

"In California, not Fiji."

"Point taken."

"What do you want to do first?" she asked.

Spend time with her. "Swim."

Addie leaned toward him, eyes bright and dancing with excitement. "How about you swim while I shower, then we switch? You shower and I go for a walk."

"You realize you came up with a plan."

She straightened. "I did, didn't I?"

"This trip will have you back to your old self before you know it."

"I'd rather be a new self."

"I don't see any need for a new you."

And he didn't. Addie was . . . special. Just the way she was.

AFTER LANDING AND a layover at Nadi International Airport, Addie and Nick boarded a floatplane. Flying on the smaller aircraft made Addie feel like she wasn't on her way to a vacation, but off on an adventure. She wiggled her toes, more excited than nervous now.

The seaplane made a pass around Starfish Island, giving her a bird's eye view of her vacation home for the next ten days. She stared in wonder at the gorgeous sights below: white beaches, several hidden among rocky coves, lush greenery and rolling hills on the island's interior and clear, blue water all around. "This is the most beautiful place I've ever seen. I need to pinch myself to make sure I'm not dreaming."

Nick leaned over her shoulder, as if wanting a better look himself. They were the only two passengers on the small plane. "Welcome to paradise, Addie. This vacation is going to be good for you."

She nodded. "I want you to enjoy this, too."

"I will."

But Fiji was nothing new to Nick. He traveled the world, working in exotic locations and staying in luxurious accommodations. There might be more sun, sand, and downtime, but the island wasn't that different from what he was used to. Still she hoped he had a good time. Maybe they could do something fun together—snorkel or fish. She missed hanging out with him.

"Starfish Island has twenty-three private beaches for you to enjoy," a fifty-something guy named Mitch, with long bleached-blond hair, said from the pilot seat. His window was partly open letting in the fresh, sea air. "The staff will help you decide which beach fits your needs best. All are secluded, but some are better suited for honeymooners."

For sex.

Mitch meant sex on the beach.

"We were hoping for some . . . privacy," Nick said.

I'm only human, babe.

She remembered what he'd said on the transpacific flight this morning. If their marriage were real, she and Nick would be making the most of those hidden coves. Swimming, kissing, making love . . .

Sexy images formed in her mind, ones starring her and Nick. Addie's cheeks warmed. She focused on the scenery below.

So what if this was their honeymoon? Sex was so not happening between them.

Not on this trip. Not ever.

Thinking about the possibility, even abstractly, was a bad idea. Like their marriage, the honeymoon wasn't real. No need to fantasize about Nick. She would only be spending enough time with him so people believed they were newlyweds, then she would let him loose to do . . .

Whatever Nick did.

All are secluded, but some are better suited for honeymooners.

Yeah, sex. Nick liked having sex. That was no secret, but he would be discreet if he met a woman and not go crazy. He enjoyed hooking up, but he wouldn't embarrass Addie. He was too good a guy to do that.

Maybe they would both meet people. Fall in love. Okay, that might be a bit much while on their honeymoon, but meeting a man and getting to know him wouldn't be bad. She hadn't dated in a long time. She wasn't sure she remembered how to flirt. Maybe Nick could give her tips and she could practice on the island. Though he'd been protective of her whenever she was around his friends.

Funny, because she'd never paid any attention to his

friends. None compared to Nick in his board shorts with water dripping down his chest and flat abs. She wet her lips.

What was the matter with her?

Nick was gorgeous, but a heartbreaker. Being friends had been the safer choice then. Being friends was the only choice now.

"We'll be landing in a minute," Mitch announced.

Her excitement grew. "I can't wait."

"When was your last vacation?" Nick asked her.

"Cancun."

His eyebrows knotted. "Our high school graduation trip?"

"I started taking care of my grandmother my freshman year of college."

"That's right." He got a faraway look in his eyes. "Cancun was a fun trip."

Except he hadn't kissed her like she thought he would. Oh, well . . . Based on the wedding kiss, she hadn't missed anything. "Fun until you told me you'd enlisted in the army and would be leaving the next week."

His tight squeeze on her shoulders brushed aside the memories and gave her more than a thrill. A heat sparked low in her belly. Maybe a goodbye kiss between friends wouldn't have been so bad.

Uh-oh. What was going on? She needed to stop thinking about kissing. *Honeymoon in name only, remember?* She couldn't lose herself in a fantasy.

"Sorry," he said. "But that seemed like the right time to tell you."

"I needed to know. That was as good a time as any." Addie looked down at the clear, blue water. She wanted to put the past behind her, be someone different, someone new, someone off on an exciting adventure. If not a real marriage and honeymoon, then another kind of beginning . . .

Time to focus on the present—a paradise full of beaches and sun and fruity drinks with paper umbrellas. She could swim and sail and participate in the forty-seven other activities the resort offered or read one of the novels she'd brought.

"What are you thinking?" Nick asked.

"That I deserve this lovely island." She raised her chin, buoyed by a resolve she hadn't felt in . . . years. "I'm going to make the most of the next ten days. Let my hair down and dance in the sand. Who knows when I'll get to do something like this again?"

Nick's eyes darkened, turning serious. Something rare for him. He started to speak then stopped himself.

"Your turn," she said. "What are you thinking?"

"This is only our first vacation. You're not going to have to wait another nine years for another one, okay?"

The raw emotion in his voice sounded nothing like the Nick she knew, but the determination behind each word warmed her heart. "Okay."

The plane landed and motored across the water toward a

long wooden dock that led to a pristine curved strip of white sand beach. Two paddleboards lay by the shore's edge. Palm fronds blew in the wind.

Her breath caught in her throat. "It's like a postcard."

"Only better. This is real life. The island is ours for the next week and a half." Nick motioned to the people on the dock. "Looks like we have a welcoming committee. Show off your pearly whites. I see cameras."

A group of people milled about, some dressed in matching blue shirts and white shorts—the resort uniform, perhaps?—and others in tropical shirts and shorts.

Addie looked down at her cutoff capri-length sweats and Dollar Store flip-flops. Comfortable, yes, but not fashionable. She sighed. "I should have put on different clothes while we were at the airport."

"You look fine."

"Says the guy who looks like a model for a Nautica photo shoot in your polo shirt and shorts."

He grinned. "Our new clothes will be waiting for us at our room. You can change when we get there."

The pilot cut the engine. "Enjoy your stay on Starfish Island. We locals like to think of this place as a tiny slice of heaven on earth."

Addie would agree.

The plane's small door opened. They stepped outside. A fresh breeze blew across her skin and played with the ends of her hair. Waves lapped against the dock, a sound she knew well but held a different echo here, like the air was lighter. Music played on the beach. Two men strummed guitars surrounded by colorfully dressed singers.

Warmth pooled in her head and heart. Who was she kidding? She felt warm all over.

The hours of travel had transported Addie to another world, to a place where she could escape reality and relax. The problems and troubles of the past no longer mattered. Her entire body felt as if it were smiling. "Wow! We're not in San Diego any longer."

Nick stood next to her, a wide smile on his face. "Don't think about San Diego while we're here."

Good advice she intended on following. She wouldn't think about anything but what was happening right now.

A woman dressed in a long blue dress held flower leis. "*Ni Sa Bula.*"

"That's the way they say welcome in Fiji," Addie whispered to Nick. "*Bula* is less formal."

He motioned to a camera crew. Two men carried cameras. A third had sound gear. "Maybe we'll get a DVD to take home."

"I want pictures, video, whatever they've got. I want to remember every minute of this vacation."

"Excited?"

She tapped her toes. "Yes."

He leaned closer. "It's going to get better."

Anticipation spurted through her. Addie felt free, no

rules to follow, no one needing her, nothing holding her back. She couldn't wait to experience everything the island offered.

A man in a white button-up short sleeve shirt and ivory shorts stepped forward. His bleached-blond hair added to his monochrome look. "Welcome to Starfish Island, Mr. and Mrs. Cahill. I'm Brad Hammond with Winning Star Productions."

His name wasn't familiar, but Addie knew no one in Fiji except Nick.

"Our production company sponsored the honeymoon contest you won." Brad's blinding smile must have taken three boxes of whitening strips. "We know this is a special time for you. The crew and I will be as inconspicuous as possible during your stay. You'll have at least an hour or two of private time each day, but we need to make sure we have enough footage to put together the show."

Private time. Footage. Show. What in the world was going on?

Nick's questioning gaze met hers. She answered with a shrug.

"We knew promotional photos would be taken," Nick said. "But a film crew . . ."

Brad held up his hand. "I understand. You're honeymooners. You want privacy before we start filming the reality show."

Reality show? Her heart pounded against her chest,

booming like the drums on the beach. Every nerve ending stood at attention. "We got married yesterday and . . ."

"Flew all night." Nick scratched his chin covered with a layer of sexy stubble from not shaving this morning. "We had no idea about the filming, uh, starting right away."

Addie appreciated Nick stepping in, even if he had no idea what was going on.

A sheepish expression crossed Brad's face. "You read the fine print."

She didn't think he meant the safety information card on the airplane. Maybe this was the missing paperwork Nick had mentioned to Emily.

"Fine," Brad relented. "We shouldn't be filming today. But the network is excited about the honeymoon reality show's potential. Sponsors are expressing interest based on your profiles. We want to send them early footage."

Nick was movie star handsome. She understood his appeal. He'd led an exciting life full of action and adventure. Unlike her.

Until a few months ago, her life had been spectacularly boring. Not that being homeless was that exciting. She'd lived day to day, reacting. Always . . . reacting. Even now. "Why are they excited?"

"An Army vet marries his childhood best friend," Brad said. "Viewers are going to fall in love with you."

Oh, no. Addie's heart dropped to her feet. Splat against the dock. She was afraid to look down for fear of seeing a bloody mess.

So much for being warm all over. An icy feeling settled in her legs. She balled her hands, a mixture of anxiety, frustration, fear and shame. Lying about their marriage to a few people in San Diego and Nick's boss was one thing, but going on TV and pretending to be honeymooners in love?

She opened her mouth to speak, but had no idea what to say. She couldn't tell the truth, not with Nick's job at stake. She couldn't scream at the injustice of being forced into more lies. Correction, the same lie, only bigger with an audience who would be watching and commenting and judging. Addie pressed her lips together. Maybe that would keep her from throwing up or blurting out what was going on.

Her vacation in paradise had been turned into ten days in hell. No resting, no relaxing, no fun. Was this karma for taking the honeymoon prize away from an in-love-newlywed couple? She didn't want to know the answer.

"Viewers might get mad at me." Nick put his arm around Addie and pulled her close. The pounding of his heart matched her own. The heat emanating from his body raised her core temperature. Sweat pooled between her breasts. She needed to take off her sweatshirt.

Time to put some distance between them. She tried to move, but he held her tightly.

"I took so long to marry her." He brushed his lips over her hair.

No. No. No. Those feathery kisses felt way too good.

What was Nick doing?

Her insides trembled over his willingness to go along with the charade for the film crew. Okay, his job was at stake. She had no doubt he could play the dutiful groom for the camera. He'd faced far worse situations, life-threatening ones where he'd been shot.

Addie wasn't like him. Sure, she had strengths. She was a good caregiver and friend, but she'd spent the past nine years hiding her emotions and feelings, always appearing upbeat for her grandmother. Not easy, but a camera hadn't been recording every facial expression and nuance. A television audience would figure out she and Nick weren't in love.

"I knew Addie was something special back when we were climbing on the monkey bars at recess," Nick continued.

"The monkey bars. That's awesome." Brad motioned the cameraman closer. "When did you fall in love?"

Oh, no. Knees weak, she leaned against Nick hoping for an ounce of his strength to fortify her. The man was solid, all muscle and confidence. But she doubted he could pull off this line of questioning with his usual pizzazz.

Nick pulled her closer like a caring husband would. "I've loved Addie for as long as I can remember. I proposed to her for the first time when we were in kindergarten."

His words—totally true—chased away the cold and chills. She loved him the same way he loved her . . . as friends. Always had. Well, when she hadn't been crushing on him, wishing she could be his girlfriend. Boy, she'd been so young and naïve back then.

"What was your answer?" Brad asked her.

"Yes," she admitted. "Though Miss Jones, our kindergarten teacher, made us promise not to kiss. She didn't want germs spread."

"I remember Miss Jones." Nick smiled. "She had a brown rabbit."

"Cocoa."

"We used to take turns bringing Cocoa home."

"Not me. Grammy didn't want rodents in the house."

"You visited Cocoa at my house."

Addie nodded. "We fed her carrots."

"I made you clean up the rabbit poop."

She laughed. "You always made me do the dirty work."

He winked. "Still do."

Brad beamed, doubling the high-power wattage of his smile. "Looks like we picked the right couple."

"Picked?" Her gazed bounced like a cat trying to catch a laser pointer. "We won the contest."

"Same thing," Brad explained. "The winning couple needed to appeal to the masses, otherwise the show would be a ratings bust."

"Someone looked over the entries and choose us, rather than selecting a random winner?" she asked.

"The selection process was explained in the rules and agreement you signed with your entry."

Nick inhaled sharply.

She forced herself from doing the same thing. Neither had read any paperwork. No rules or agreements had been signed. Emily had filled out the entry form, included pictures of them, and forged their signatures. Addie and Nick hadn't known about the contest until they'd been declared the winners and asked to provide social security numbers for tax purposes.

Stupid? Maybe.

But no one turned down a free ten-day vacation complete with new wardrobes. Maybe they should have asked questions, made sure there weren't any catches to the prize like starring in a reality TV program.

Brad's gaze narrowed to slits. "Is there a problem?"

"No problem." Nick's smile didn't crinkle the corner of his eyes, but no one would notice except her. "We would appreciate the allowed time alone. We haven't had a wedding night yet."

Nick was trying to buy them time, but her cheeks burned. Did everything have to be about sex when you were on your honeymoon? Still she managed a smile and a nod.

"No worries." Brad held out his hands palms facing them. "We'll film you carrying your bride over the threshold of the *bure* and then leave you alone. Jet lag won't make for good footage anyway."

"That works." Nick's voice sounded forced, like he was talking between clenched teeth. "Doesn't it, honey?"

The endearment surprised her. He'd called her many things over the years, but never anything intimate. This was going to take some getting used to.

"Sounds good to me." She'd rather be dealing with cramps. Okay, not really, but she wanted to enjoy her first real vacation in over a decade, not play an in-love newlywed couple for the camera with her best guy friend when her heart wished she was here with her one true love, whoever that might be.

"Let's go," Brad said. "The sooner we get the footage. The sooner the two of you can be alone."

Nick dropped his arm from around her. "We're ready."

"Our overnight bags?" she asked.

"They will be delivered to the *bure*," Brad said. "A little advice to make things easier. Ignore the cameras, pretend they're not there, and most importantly, be yourselves."

This wasn't going to work. If she and Nick acted like themselves, everyone would know they weren't in love.

She wanted to be someone different, someone new, someone off on an exciting adventure.

Why had she thought that on the seaplane?

Nick held her hand. "Come on."

She laced her fingers with his, trying to keep her hand from tensing too much, and walked next to him.

He lowered his mouth to her ear. "I'll figure a way out of this."

She wasn't sure how he would, but she clung to his

words the way she gripped his hand.

"Trust me," he whispered. "It's going to be okay, babe."

The word babe bristled. Addie preferred being called honey. She didn't like being lumped in with the long list of women he called babe, ones he'd dated and left. She wasn't like them.

Her dad had deserted her and her mom when Addie was a toddler. Her mother had dumped her at her grandparents when she was four. Her aunt and mother had evicted her after her grandmother's death. Addie had no one to call family now, but she had Nick.

She knew he would never desert her. He might not be perfect, they might not have seen each other much these past nine years, but his friendship was like the sun, always there. Constant. No matter if the sky was blue or overcast.

Forget Prince Charming. She wouldn't want to be on Starfish Island with anyone else. Nick would figure a way out of this reality TV mess and make everything better.

The way he had in the past. The way he always would.

Chapter Three

NICK'S FEET SOUNDED against the path, his steps heavier than Addie's who walked next to him. He kept a smile on his face for the camera, but inside he seethed. What in the hell had Emily been thinking when she entered them in the contest?

He was a personal security professional. He didn't want the public profile that went with being on a reality TV show. Incognito was the way he lived when he was enlisted and now that he was out.

Worse, hadn't Emily considered how this would affect Addie? A friend should know better. She'd been through so much with her grandmother's illness, the death, and the subsequent battle over the house. Addie needed looking after, not put on display for millions of viewers' guilty pleasure.

He would text Emily while he determined how to extract Addie from this situation. Sure, he could take out the entire film crew. Given their frat boy looks, spray-on tans, and underwear model physiques, the odds were in Nick's favor even though he was outnumbered four to one. Too bad Addie would never condone violence.

That meant figuring out another way to get her off the island in the next twenty-four hours—sickness, food poisoning, death of a friend or loved one, an impending lawsuit. The last one wasn't much of a stretch given Addie's family stealing her inheritance and breaking her heart.

Yes, he could come up with an exit strategy and whisk her to safety. That was why he was paid the big bucks, but he needed time to call and make arrangements. Until then, he would keep holding Addie's hand, being her husband, and making sure she didn't get too upset.

She shouldn't worry. No laws were being broken. They were legally married. What did it matter if they didn't plan to live as husband and wife and share a bed?

They were good friends who got along better than some married couples he knew. They had kept in touch for the last nine years when he'd drifted away from most other civilians, including his parents. He and Addie had looked out for each other from the time they were little kids, through good times and bad. So what if sex wasn't part of their marriage? There wasn't another woman he respected more.

Playing a dutiful, crazy about his bride newlywed until they left the island would be a breeze. Though his gut told him holding hands and staring into each other's eyes wasn't going to be enough for the cameras. Newlyweds kissed and touched each other.

In full disclosure, Nick wouldn't mind doing either. Once he'd almost kissed her, but chickened out at the last second. Fear of losing her friendship had stopped him.

Since then, things had changed. They'd changed. But their friendship hadn't changed.

Addie had hesitated before the kiss during the wedding. Understandable. A physical relationship wasn't part of their agreement. He'd made the kiss brief, hoping not to raise suspicions with Emily. Nick would do the same thing with the film crew. He didn't want Addie forced into doing something because a camera was pointed at them. She looked stressed enough.

Her pasted-on smile couldn't hide the *V* between her brows, deeper than he'd ever seen, including when he'd picked up her, two suitcases and three boxes from Emily's apartment. Addie had blinked back tears when they moved her into his townhome. She'd been through so much and kept trying to be strong. Being on a TV show and forced to act like an in-love bride was the last thing she needed.

"Shouldn't be much farther," he said.

Addie looked up at him. Her ponytail bounced, the movement as comforting as a welcoming wave from an old friend. "I'm good."

Nick gave her hand a reassuring squeeze, his way of telling Addie he was here for her. He would take care of her the way she'd taken care of him during his parents' fights, their divorce and his deployments. That was what friends did for one another.

She rewarded him with a shy smile.

A smile was good. They would get through this. Maybe have a good laugh about their escape from reality TV once they were back in San Diego.

Brad grinned. The dude had the whitest teeth Nick had ever seen. Unnaturally white. Weird. Glow in the dark?

"You okay?" Addie whispered, her breath warm against his skin.

Always thinking about others.

"Fine." Nick focused on her small hand in his. He hadn't realized how petite she was. She'd acted so strong and brave when they were growing up she seemed taller. "Everything's going to be fine."

A large woman wearing a long blue dress greeted them outside their *bure*, a thatched roof cottage surrounded by palm trees and sand. "Welcome, welcome. I am Lani, your *bure* Mama. Call me Mama Lani. I will see to all your needs while you are on Starfish Island. You will have the most romantic honeymoon ever."

"Thank you." Addie's voice sounded weak, tired.

"Oh, child, come to Mama Lani." The woman enveloped Addie in a big hug. "You are exhausted. A wedding, travel. You need a bath, then a rest."

"It's been a long day," Nick agreed.

Mama Lani patted his arm. Nothing more than a slight

touch, but the woman exuded warmth and kindness, reminding him of his Aunt Eliza who never judged him like his parents had, but showered him with affection, attention, and little presents from the Dollar Store.

"We need to shoot a few scenes first," Brad said.

Mama Lani frowned. "One scene. Then you go."

Nick liked Lani. A lot.

"Come see your *bure* for the next ten days. You will like it. Your clothes arrived before you and are unpacked. A staff member will deliver your overnight bags shortly."

The camera crew followed, directed by a still smiling Brad. Didn't the guy's facial muscles get tired? Botox injections? He seemed too young for those.

At the entrance, Brad cleared his throat. "Threshold."

Nick wanted the film crew gone. He swept Addie into his arms.

She inhaled sharply. "What—?"

"A husband carries his bride over the threshold, remember?" He hadn't done this at his townhome after the ceremony. The thought hadn't crossed his mind. Wedding traditions weren't on his need-to-know list. But he liked how Addie felt against him, soft in all the right places.

"Don't hurt your back," she cautioned.

He couldn't tell whether she was teasing or serious. Her voice sounded lighthearted, but her eyes darkened. He flashed a grin. "You're not heavy."

Addie had curves he liked feeling. She wore modest

43

clothes—baggy ones—that did nothing to stimulate the male imagination, but he remembered what she looked like in a bikini. Her image had fueled his teenaged fantasies until he learned to push them away. Like he should now with her hips pressing against his abdomen waking different parts of his anatomy.

He carried Addie into the *bure* to the sitting area with an L-shaped couch and rattan coffee table. The inside was bright, open with a bedroom toward the back and a patio in front. A ceiling fan circulated the air, providing a light breeze.

Nick placed Addie on the bamboo floor. "Welcome to paradise, Mrs. Cahill."

Pink tinged her cheeks. She looked up at him through her eyelashes. "Thanks . . . sweetie."

Aw, so cute. Nick kissed the top of her hand. "My pleasure."

Mama Lani released a loud sigh, then clapped her hands once. The sound echoed through the room. "That's enough."

She shooed the film crew out of the *bure*. The four men left without a word. Brad typed on his tablet as he walked out.

"Thank you," Nick said to their new friend.

"You rest." Mama Lani took Addie by the hand. "I take care of your beautiful bride."

His muscles tightened. "I want to stay with her."

"It's okay." Addie said with a soft smile. "I'm tired. Must be jetlag. I could use some help."

Help she hadn't received in the last nine years. A knot in his stomach tightened, grew. Her so-called family, nothing but selfish, money grubbing, entitled jerks, had put Addie through hell before and after her grandmother's death.

At least she had Mama Lani here.

That might make up for the film crew.

Then again . . .

"Beer is in the bar," Mama Lani said, leading Addie away.

Nick did a quick surveillance of the *bure*, checking for hidden cameras and microphones. He didn't trust many people and wouldn't let his guard down around strangers, especially a film crew from a reality TV show.

Paranoid? Maybe.

Satisfied the *bure* was clean, Nick found the bar. Beer filled the mini fridge. "Now we're talking."

With a bottle in hand, he walked out to the patio. A breeze carried the scent of salt and flowers, a nice combination. To his left was a day bed, large enough to fit two. He'd sleep here and give Addie the bed inside. On the right, a hammock hung between two palm trees.

With a pull from the bottle, he sauntered over and lay down. "This is what I call a vacation."

The only thing missing was Addie. Nick hoped she was okay without him. He had to admit Mama Lani was a better person to draw Addie's bath and help her undress. Though he was up for the job if need be. He took another drink.

Better not think about a naked Addie.

Holding her a few minutes ago had awakened dormant feelings, ones he'd buried back in high school. Addie was his friend, not some woman he wanted to hook up with then forget about.

Nick wasn't like a dragon that hadn't been fed for over a decade. He knew how to handle attraction, push aside the feelings, as he'd always done. Addie would never know what he was thinking. He drank more beer.

If only dealing with the film crew would be as easy. But an extraction plan was forming in his mind. Until they were out of here, Nick would do what he could to keep the cameras away. Addie would be safe. Nothing would happen to her. Not on his watch.

THE THICK, LUXURIOUS cotton robe brushed Addie's moisturized skin. She'd never felt more pampered after taking a long, relaxing soak in a bubble filled tub then rinsing off in a waterfall shower built for two. Yet the conch-shell sized knot of worry in the pit of her stomach hadn't been washed away.

She'd had crushes, dated, lusted and been in a relation-ship her freshman year of college until she had to drop out of school, but not once had she ever experienced the I-want-to-wake-up-next-to-you-every-morning-even-though-your-breath-is-foul kind of love, an everlasting love, the kind of love she'd dreamed about . . . forever.

Being carried over the threshold in Nick's arms gave her a glimpse of what that might be like. She wanted more. She wanted to find true love. She wanted the happily ever after.

If she and Nick . . .

Stop. Now.

Getting caught up in the make-believe would complicate everything. They were pretending, nothing more would happen. End of story.

Hanging out and being roommates had sounded easy enough, but Nick's marriage plan had strings she hadn't counted on. Addie needed to be careful. She might not be free for the next five years to find her Mr. Right, but that didn't mean she should transfer her longing to Nick. Sure, she'd been in love with him before. Most girls at school had. But then, like now, she knew dating him would be bad, disastrous, worst idea ever.

"You look better. More relaxed." A big, warm smile spread across Mama Lani's face, making Addie yearn for another hug. The woman's hugs gave a sense of belonging and home, two things she hadn't felt in months. "You'll have to make sure your husband eats dinner. Mr. Nick won't be able to take his eyes off you tonight."

"I'm a yoga pants and oversized T-shirt kind of girl." Caring for her grandmother took too much time and money for Addie to be into fashion. She might have felt invisible to the opposite sex during that time, but comfortable and cheap continued to be Addie's motto. "Nick doesn't mind. Besides, he's going to be tired. All he'll want to do is eat, then go to bed."

"He's napping on the hammock outside. Even if he's still tired, I'll make sure he stays awake." Mama Lani pointed to a light pink cocktail dress hanging on a bathroom hook. "There'll be no drowsy eyes while you're wearing that."

Addie's breath caught in her throat. "Oh, how gorgeous."

"The color will be flattering on you."

She touched the fabric. Soft, shimmery, light. So lovely. The dress was like nothing she'd worn or could afford. "This is mine?"

Mama Lani nodded. "You have an entire closet full of clothes as beautiful as this. Whoever chose your wardrobe did a wonderful job with the colors and styles."

"Wow." Addie hadn't worn something this nice since splurging on a prom dress her senior year of high school. "This is some honeymoon prize."

"There's lingerie, too." Mama Lani handed her a pair of pink lace panties, wispy as spun sugar. "Lots of frilly things for you to wear."

Addie stared at the sexy panties as if the lace were radioactive. Multi-colored hipsters were her standard fare, paired with sensible bras. She didn't own a scrap of lace. Her only thong, a gag gift from Emily one Christmas, had been tossed in the back of a dresser drawer. Too much or rather, too little, for Addie to wear for herself.

These new panties were a novelty. A challenge. A chance to step outside her normal self and be another woman, an adventurous one who showered under a waterfall and wore shimmering fabrics over delicate lace. A part of her couldn't wait. But the other part was . . . hesitant. Uncertain. Overwhelmed.

Addie wrapped her arms across her churning stomach, then leaned back against the counter.

Mama Lani was at Addie's side in an instant. "What's wrong?"

A pain formed behind her forehead. She massaged her temples, but that didn't help. This was a mental ache, not a physical one. "I'm not used to dressing up in fancy clothes or wearing make-up. Ponytails are my normal hairstyle. All this is so strange. I'm a little scared."

Anxiety spiraled. An invisible weight pressed on her chest. She struggled for air. Everything about this trip was out of her comfort level. She'd never spent this much time with Nick, not even when they were kids. Sure, she'd moved into the guest room at his townhouse, but since that night she hadn't seen him until the morning of their wedding.

Nothing she could do about Nick, but the pink dress . . . Beautiful, except a beach towel provided the same coverage, maybe more. "I'm not sure I can pull off this kind of style. I've never worn anything strapless. I'm going to look . . .

awkward."

"You're a beautiful woman with a stunning trousseau." Mama Lani patted Addie's shoulder. "You will look lovely, not awkward. Once you put on the dress, you'll see how good you feel. And your husband will enjoy undressing you."

The thought of Nick unzipping her dress brought a smile. Uh-no. She pressed her lips together. Unless the zipper broke, the guy was not touching her clothing.

"Look at yourself." Mama Lani turned her so they faced the mirror. "You have a perfect complexion. No foundation is necessary."

Addie focused on her reflection. "But the freckles—

"Add character."

She'd never thought of her freckles that way. They'd always been something she wanted to hide or go away. "Character is good I suppose."

"Very good. You have lovely features and beautiful hazel green eyes," Mama Lani pointed out. "You don't need much make-up. Some blush to bring out your cheekbones and a touch of mascara to highlight your long lashes."

"I didn't pack make-up, only lip gloss."

"Cosmetics were provided with the new wardrobe."

"The contest thought of everything."

Mama Lani nodded. "I have friends who can teach you about make-up and help me with your hair. No ponytail tonight."

"It's nice of you to offer, but that's not your job."

"I'm your mama *bure*. Let me mama you."

Warmth flowed through Addie. She felt special and cared for, a way she hadn't felt since her grandmother's stroke nine years ago. They'd switched roles overnight. Addie had been a freshman on a full-ride scholarship with a boyfriend, first semester finals behind her, but that changed in an instant. She'd had to change. No more going out and having fun when her grandmother needed constant care and bills paid.

"Sure. I'd like that very much." Maybe having the film crew following them didn't have to ruin her time here. Maybe having Mama Lani around could salvage the vacation. Maybe Addie could have fun, something she'd missed having for so long. And, of course, there was Nick. Face-to-face time would be nice. She straightened her shoulders. "Guess it's makeover time."

NICK WOKE TO a chorus singing. Not people, birds. The sound carried on the sea breeze and settled on the palm fronds above him. He lifted himself onto his elbows, staring through the greenery to the waves rolling to shore. The hammock swung back and forth, tempting him to close his eyes and go back to sleep.

Something hummed. Not a bird. An engine.

Adrenaline sent him out of the hammock and to his feet in one fluid movement. Every muscle tensed, on alert and ready to act.

He scanned the periphery, looking for anything threatening or out of the ordinary. Nothing in close range.

On the water, a pontoon boat motored. The driver wore the blue and white resort uniform. A couple, his passengers, wore swimsuits and laughed, their arms linked around each other's waists.

No threat. Nick's pulse slowed.

Vacation. Time to relax, not work. But his job was protecting those around him. Turning off those instincts didn't just happen when he felt responsible for Addie.

Something rustled behind him.

He spun.

Mama Lani stood in the doorway to the *bure.* "Addie is finished, Mr. Nick."

He swiped his empty beer bottle from the ground, then went inside. Quiet, except for the fan. He didn't see Addie. The hair at the back of his neck stiffened. "Where is she?"

"Off being pampered."

"Addie needs to be spoiled while she's on Starfish Island."

Mama Lani eyed him warily. "Your bride deserves to be spoiled no matter where she is, including home."

"That's what I plan to do," he said quickly, feeling defensive. If asked to pick sides, Mama Lani had Team Addie written all over her. "But we're here now."

"Towels are in the bathroom along with a robe and an

outfit to complement Addie's dress."

Starfish Island was known for their service and so far he wasn't disappointed. He'd never been one for lounging outside the bedroom, but he could get used to this. "Thanks. I appreciate you taking such good care of us, especially Addie. She's been through a rough time."

"Then it's good she has both of us."

Nick nodded, but unease coiled in his gut. He'd been out of the country when Addie's grandmother died, and her life fell apart. She hadn't contacted him right away, or he would have paid the funeral expenses and given her a place to stay. At least he could help her now. An image of Addie asleep on the plane formed. So sweet and vulnerable. He would make sure no one took advantage or hurt her again.

"Once you're ready, go to the dock on the right side of the *bure*. That's where dinner will be served." Mischief gleamed in Mama Lani's dark eyes. "I have something special for your first meal together in paradise."

"Can't wait. I'm starving."

She grinned wryly. "I promise tonight will more than satisfy your appetite."

Nick showered, then put on a tropical print button down and linen tan pants. He stared at the clothes hanging in the armoire—polo shirts, T-shirts, button downs, shorts, pants, a lightweight cotton sports coat—giving kudos to whoever purchased his wardrobe. High-quality and stylish resort clothes.

By the time he arrived at the dock, the sun was sinking into the horizon. Streaks of blue, pink and purple painted the sky. The temperature had dropped a few degrees.

Lanterns illuminated the way. At the end of the dock, flames from three torches reflected in the water. More lanterns, sitting on the dock between the poles, provided a soft glow of light for a table set for two. Tropical flowers filled a vase placed on a white linen cloth. Flickering candlelight danced. Waves rolled against the dock with a soothing, rhythmic sound.

So romantic. Exactly what a newlywed couple would enjoy. Especially a blushing bride like Addie.

Nick tugged on the neckline of his shirt. Not the time to get caught up in the trappings of hearts, flowers, and violins. He knew better. A fake marriage with Addie had a better chance of succeeding than a real one like his parents'.

Heels clicked against the dock.

He glanced toward the shore.

A woman walked toward him with flowers braided in her long, curly brown hair.

His mouth went dry. Stunning was the only word to describe her.

She wore a sexy light pink dress. The strapless bodice showed off firm, round breasts and a trim waist. The skirt clung to her hips then flared, flowing around her thighs and falling well above her knees. Strappy silver sandals accentuated long, slim legs.

He took a closer look at her face, did a double take, choked on a breath, coughed. "Addie?"

"Mama Lani went all out tonight."

Hot damn. "Look at you. Smokin'."

She spun around, sending her skirt flying up. A peek of her pink lace panties sent his temperature soaring as if a solar flare had exploded inside him.

"You like?" she asked.

"Very much."

Addie smoothed the sexy dress. "The style is different from what I usually wear."

"Suits you. Let's you shine."

But the dress was only part of the package. She wore make-up. Eye shadow and mascara, a touch of blush, nothing crazy. Her pink glossy lips looked full and kissable. He wanted to know if she tasted as good as she—

"Nick?"

"Enjoying the view."

Her cheeks reddened, but her gaze didn't waver. She struck a pose, one that raised the hem of her skirt. "Look all you want."

Sassy. He liked that. "I plan to."

"Mama Lani's friends helped me get ready, showed me make-up tricks and new styles for my hair."

Her excitement bubbled over. About time her eyes twinkled again. "Sounds like fun."

"It was." She shimmied her shoulders, giving a bounce to

her breasts and making him wonder what they would look like free and in the palms of his hands. "The ladies made me feel like Cinderella getting ready for the ball."

"You look like a princess."

She beamed. Her million-dollar smile made the long flight and whatever they had to put up with from the film crew worth the trouble. Might as well make the best of their evening while they were here.

"Thanks," she said.

"Thank you." He motioned for her to spin again. She did, but not fast enough to make her skirt fly up. Damn. He'd wanted another peek. "Looks like I've gone and married myself a trophy wife."

"Yeah, right." She winked. Her playfulness made him want to skip dinner and go straight to dessert . . . between the sheets. "You look handsome yourself."

Anticipation prickled. She'd never called him that.

"Love the shirt," she added.

The shirt had pastel tropical flowers with larger tan ones in the foreground. The pink ones matched her dress. "Mama Lani said we'd coordinate."

Addie nodded, her hair swaying. "We do. Like real honeymooners."

A real honeymoon with his wife sounded perfect. A wedding night in a tropical paradise deserved a night of hot sex.

Crap, what was he thinking? This was Addie. Sex wasn't part of their agreement. But that didn't change the fact he wanted her.

Whoa. Time to slow down.

Nick looked around. Where was the waiter? He needed a drink. Whiskey. Straight.

She shifted her weight between her feet.

His gaze dropped to the pair of sexy, strappy silver heels she wore. Her toenail color matched her dress. "Love the shoes."

"I practiced walking. I'm not used to heels." She pointed her toe, showing off her toned calf muscle. "Most people go barefoot around here, but Mama Lani said I should wear the shoes because you would like them."

"I do." More than he should, but he couldn't help himself. Her eagerness appealed to him at a gut level. She'd been locked away for the past nine years, and Mama Lani had used her key. Or maybe the island had. He liked thinking he might have given the door a shove. "If your feet hurt, tell me. You can take off your shoes, and I'll carry you back to the *bure*."

Holding her would be sweet torture, but he was willing and able. Who was he kidding? Nick would gladly take off her shoes, her dress, her panties.

He swallowed. Thoughts like that would get him into trouble. Addie was his wife in name only. She'd never treated him as anything other than her friend, good old Nick.

They'd never crossed the line though he'd been tempted once or twice. Any romantic interest was in the past. He had to be careful, not impose on Addie, but let her know how special she was. "Carrying you won't be a problem. You deserve VIP treatment. Very important princesses do."

"That's so sweet of you." The sincerity in her voice matched the smile on her face. "But I can walk barefoot if my feet hurt. Crossing fingers they don't."

"You had a French manicure." He reached for her fingers, raised them to his mouth, kissed the top of her hand then let go. "You smell different."

Her cheeks deepened two shades of pink. She stared at her hands. "That's the lotion Mama Lani gave me. Lotus something or other. Made my skin tingle."

"Nice scent." Everything about Addie was nice. He pulled out a chair and motioned for her to sit. "A seat for the beautiful princess to keep her feet from hurting."

She curtsied, then sat. "Everything is so lovely. I wonder what's on the menu tonight."

"I'd say fish."

A boring reply, but Nick had forced himself not to make a flirty reply about wanting her. He joked with Addie via text and email. She had a great sense of humor and didn't mind his off-color jokes or military-inspired humor. But letting the sexual innuendos fly tonight might get him into trouble.

Her appearance wasn't the only attraction. Seeing her relax and have fun was sexy, too. The *V* above her nose wasn't as deep. She hadn't reached the carefree stage, but she was closer than she'd been in a long while. That pleased

Nick. He sat across from her.

A waiter arrived with champagne and two flutes.

Finally. Nick would prefer whiskey or a beer, but he wasn't going to turn down a bottle of bubbly.

The waiter handed Addie a glass, his gaze lingering on her longer than Nick liked. "Compliments of Brad."

She flashed Nick a closed-mouthed smile. So beautiful.

"At least the guy's good for something," Nick muttered, taking his glass from the waiter and wishing the man would leave them alone. He wasn't jealous. No way. But he was protective. Yeah, that was it. Protective over his friend. Make that his *wife*.

A memory rushed back. When he was younger, his friends had called him Addie's husband. They joked about him being in love with her. He countered he'd needed to protect her because she was like a sister. Except as they went through high school, his feelings toward her weren't brotherly.

They weren't now, either.

She didn't seem to notice the attention from the waiter or Nick. She focused on her surroundings. He didn't blame her. This might be an all-inclusive resort, but Mama Lani deserved a special tip for setting the romantic atmosphere with this meal and helping Addie get ready.

"I'll be back with a platter of appetizers and to tell you about the dinner choices." The waiter placed the champagne bottle in an ice bucket, then walked down the dock toward the beach.

"To new adventures." She raised her glass, a twinkle in her eyes. "May our ten days turn out better than we expect."

Damn. Nick rubbed his fingers against the flute. "About the ten days. I was thinking we'd make an excuse—I have eight to choose from—then catch the first flight off the island tomorrow morning."

Her face fell. She lowered her champagne. "Oh, okay."

Only two words, but the disappointment in her voice clawed at his chest. "The reality show . . ."

"Not a good idea with your job. I get it."

"No, but . . ." He studied her face, noting the smile and twinkle had vanished. The *V* deepened again. He hadn't expected this reaction. "You want to stay with a film crew on our tails?"

She glanced around, her gaze lingering on the beach. "It may sound crazy, but I like this place. Mama Lani is so nice. I understand if we have to go. Your job is the whole reason we got married."

"We got married to help you, too." Nick didn't want her to think they'd married only for him. "Emily's couch was fine in the beginning, but you couldn't stay there forever and it's time you went back to college."

"I know, but the reality show doesn't affect me the way it will you."

He didn't understand why she wanted to stay. "The film crew made you nervous."

"They did, but I'm not sure they'll ruin paradise for me. The island is spectacular."

"Yes, but reality TV is a misnomer. The crew is going to tell us what to do and how to act, then edit the show how they want. Nothing on the show will be real."

She raised her glass toward her lips. "Nothing about our marriage is real."

"True." Addie needed time to relax and find the person she'd once been, but going home was the easy and safe choice. The list of reasons for leaving outweighed those for staying. "I don't want you to be uncomfortable."

"I'm uncomfortable lying about our marriage. That's going to be the case whether we're here or in San Diego."

Her words surprised him. "You've thought about this."

"I'm thinking it out now."

"You want to stay."

"Only if you do."

Nick should be happy she'd left the choice to him, but he didn't want to disappoint her. If she wanted to stay, he would figure out a way to make this work for Addie and for him. "Okay. We're staying."

She leaned forward. "Are you sure?"

He would talk to his boss, determine out what could be said about his job and what couldn't. No last names used or anything about him working in personal security. He'd limit the information about his military career. No one needed to know he'd been on an ODA team, better known to the public as an A-Team. Special Forces would be good enough, the U.S. Army better.

Nick tapped his glass against hers. The chime hung in the air, a perfect pitch to match their perfect evening. "I'm positive."

Chapter Four

LIGHT HIT ADDIE'S face. Morning already? Last night, she'd put on a frilly white nightie and climbed into bed. She didn't remember anything else. No doubt sleep had come hard and fast. Being a princess for the evening was tiring work, especially combined with jetlag, excitement, worry, and champagne.

She blinked open her eyes, raised her head slightly, looking at the hand-woven ceiling and the sheer white curtains hanging on sides of the bed. The muted sound of a ceiling fan was all she could hear.

So quiet and peaceful.

Nowhere to be. No one to worry about. No one to accuse her of stealing her grandmother's cottage.

A feeling of contentment settled over her. She loved everything about Starfish Island: the *bure*, Mama Lani, the entire resort. Addie lay against her pillow, not tired but wanting to relish in the moment, something she hadn't felt like doing in . . . years.

Today would be her first full day of vacation. Her first full day with the film crew, too, but she wouldn't think about them. She would, however, think of Nick, her handsome in-name-only husband. She rolled onto her right side, facing the large, empty place where he would sleep if they were married for real. The covers were messed up, and the pillow had an indention mark.

Nick must have done that before heading to the patio's day bed last night or first thing this morning. He'd done a good job. Anyone looking at the king-sized bed would assume a couple had slept together. But a kiss on the forehead was the only wedding night action after a spectacular and romantic dinner on the dock.

For the best.

She and Nick were friends, good friends. They might not have spent much time together lately, but they'd picked up without missing a beat—talking, joking, flirting the way they had back in high school. She'd managed to keep her shoes on the entire evening, too, and hadn't needed carrying. An omen they could pull this off honeymoon-marriage sham? She hoped so.

Things were going so well she would believe almost anything. Naïve? Yes, but this was her vacation on a fantasy island. She was willing to forget reality. Last night, she'd felt sixteen again with a life full of possibilities ahead of her. Nick had made her feel comfortable and pretty. He'd listened when she said she wanted to stay and changed his mind about leaving. This place was paradise.

Humming the theme from Disneyland's Tiki Room, she sat. The sheet dropped to her lap. Whether their contest entry had been randomly picked or purposely chosen, she no longer cared.

Emily must have known they would have never come if she'd told them about the reality TV show. Way to skirt the issue, but then again, she was an expert at that and one reason she was so good at advertising. Still Addie owed Emily for entering their names into the contest. A honeymoon-between-friends was the perfect start to their in-name-only marriage.

Nick walked from the bathroom area, his hair wet and a towel wrapped low around his hips. "You're awake."

You're almost naked. She gulped. Nodded.

Wowza. Her gaze traveled down his muscular chest covered with tattoos to his rock solid abs. He'd had a nice body in high school, but nothing like the awe-inspiring hotness standing in front of her.

Ripped. Cut. She'd run out of adjectives to describe his amazing better-than-an-underwear-model physique before she was ready to stop looking.

Oops. No staring. Nick might get the wrong idea.

Or maybe she would.

Addie fingered the edge of the sheet, wanting to look anywhere but at him, except her gaze kept straying back to his chest, his abs and lower.

"See something you like?"

Busted. Her cheeks warmed. She needed to say something. Fast. But she'd die of embarrassment before admitting being struck by a sudden case of lust due to his killer body. "Isn't the shower great? I wondered what standing under a waterfall would feel like. Now I know."

"You should try the real thing. There might be a waterfall or two on the island. I'll ask."

She jerked her gaze up to his face, realizing she'd been distracted by his abs again. At least she could own up to what she'd been looking at. "You've been working out."

He stared at her with an interested expression. "Yeah."

"Ladies must like that."

"A side benefit. I need to be in shape for my job."

She fought the urge to cringe. The guy was a bodyguard. Working out was a job requirement. "Right. I knew that."

What was wrong with her? She hadn't drunk enough champagne to be buzzed this morning. Lust was one thing, but maybe not dating for years had taken a toll and pushed her over the edge. Gawking over Nick, her friend, in a towel would be proof. The last thing she wanted to be was one of his lovers. No way was she joining that endangered species list.

He raised an eyebrow. "Nice jammies."

"Part of the new wardrobe." One of the nightie's spaghetti straps fell off her shoulder. She pushed the thin white satin ribbon into place. "I have one for each night. A little excessive."

"Not at all." A mischievous smile spread across his face. "Looking forward to the bedtime fashion shows."

His playful tone set off a warning bell in her head. She remembered when they'd been at the beach boogie boarding. Sophomore, no, junior year. Her bikini strap had broken. He'd come to her rescue, but not before he'd gotten a look at her exposed left breast.

She glanced down. The white fabric of her nightie covered her, but was sheer, something she hadn't realized being so tired last night.

Double oops. She pulled up the sheet to her neck. "I . . ."

"You have nothing to be shy about," Nick teased. "Don't forget, I'm your husband. You're beautiful, and the nightgown is perfect for you."

Perfect for a bride on her honeymoon to entice her groom. Not perfect for a friend rooming with a friend of the opposite sex. But Nick seemed cool about this. Maybe she shouldn't be so uptight. They would be living together for the next five years. At some point she would see him in a towel again.

She loosened her grip on the sheet. "Well, I'm your wife. I don't see you prancing around naked showing off your wares."

He grabbed onto the edge of towel. "I can remedy that."

Nick wouldn't. Oh, yes, he would.

She squeezed her eyes closed and covered her head with

the sheet.

He laughed. Of course he would find this funny.

Something thudded against the bamboo floor. The towel? She saw light through the sheet but nothing else. "What was that?"

"My towel."

Her pulse kicked up a notch. Temptation flared until common sense kicked in. Naked or not, this was still Nick. "What do you think you're doing?"

"Following orders."

His body might have improved, but his sense of humor was the same. He must be grinning from ear to ear. "I was joking."

"Sure about that?"

No. Yes. Stop. No second-guessing. Nick made a habit of getting naked in front of women, and she was a woman, but that didn't mean . . . "Yes, I'm sure. Are you still naked?"

"Why don't you find out?"

He was playing with her, teasing, seeing how far he could push her. Part of Addie was amused. The other part imagined him strutting around with nothing on but a smile.

She fanned herself with her hand. "No, thank you."

"So polite."

Not exactly. The thoughts running through her head ran more to the naughty side. She swallowed. Maybe leaving the island hadn't been such a bad idea. "Nick?"

"Hmmm."

"It's warm under here."

"I'm quite comfy."

Heat rushed up her neck. "I can imagine. I mean . . ."

"What do you mean?"

"Nothing." Nine days of this would be . . . challenging. "No, there's something. I think we need, um, ground rules."

"About?"

"This."

"What?"

"Nakedness."

"Not a fan of birthday suits?"

She could tell he was smiling. "I never said that."

"When was the last time you saw a man naked?"

Addie blew out a puff of air. "A week and a half ago."

"Living a secret life I know nothing about?"

"Nothing so clandestine or exciting." Though maybe that was what she needed to keep from overreacting to Nick.

"Gotta give me more than that," he said.

"It's nothing."

"A naked guy is not nothing."

"Says the naked guy."

"Tell me."

Might as well. Maybe he'd take advantage of the time to dress. "After brunch, Emily and I stopped by to watch the surfers. We were standing right next to one guy when he changed out of his wetsuit."

"Liked what you saw?"

The man was incorrigible. "I'm not going to answer."

"Did you take any pics?"

"Ewww."

"You're right. Not your style. But Emily . . ."

Addie had taken away Emily's cell phone. Time to get this conversation back on track. Where were they? Oh, right. Ground rules. "An in-name-only, no-sex marriage probably should exclude being naked around each other."

"Probably?"

Laughter sounded in his voice. No doubt he enjoyed making Addie squirm. He was doing a good job. Not that he could see her under the sheet. "Definitely."

"Fine, as long as this rule doesn't keep me from seeing your new jammies each night. Fashion show, remember?"

"Nick . . ."

"Otherwise, nakedness shall be acceptable here. You decide."

Not much of a decision. She blew out a puff of air. "Fine. You get to see the pajamas." She'd show him the lingerie on a hanger. He'd left wiggle room for that to be okay. "Now will you get dressed?"

"I'm dressed. Have been for a while."

She groaned, but kept the sheet over her head. "Really?"

"I'm a guy. Doesn't take me long. A minute max."

Addie lowered the sheet to her chin. His royal blue swim trunks intensified the color his eyes. "You could have told me."

"And miss all the fun of a blushing bride hiding under the covers. No way."

"You are . . ."

"The best." He winked. "Get dressed. Mama Lani was setting the table on the patio when I was coming back from my run. Let's eat then hit the beach. Maybe we can sneak away before Brad and company are up."

"I wonder what I'm supposed to wear."

He motioned to his swim trunks. "A matching bikini and cover up are in the bathroom for you."

"They must think if our clothes match, we do, too."

"We match. Not romantically, but in other ways, or our friendship would have never lasted this long."

"I guess."

"It's true." He grinned wryly. "Romantic or not, we are the cutest couple on this island."

"Not going to let that die."

"Nope."

"Even if we're not a couple."

"Hey, we're a couple of good friends. That's better than two people who will divorce in a year or two and never see each other again."

"We'll be divorced in five years," she half-joked, thinking of the end date to his marriage plan.

"But after the divorce, nothing will change. You and I will still be friends." His eyes darkened. "Not many married people can say that."

Not many engaged couples, either. He didn't have to say the words for her to know he must be thinking about Carrie. Nick had never been one to get serious, but the woman had ruined him for wanting any type of long-term relationship in the future. "Never thought of the end of our fake marriage that way."

"Lots of ways to spin this." He sat on the bed. "Today when they're filming us, we may be asked to do things you're not comfortable doing with me. If that's the case, let me know. We'll figure something out."

"And if we can't . . ."

"We suck it up and do our best."

"That's what I was afraid you'd say."

Nick touched her shoulder, his hand warm against her skin. "Listen, no matter what happens in front of the camera, nothing changes between us. We're friends, Addie. Single, married, divorced. No matter what, we'll always be friends. No stupid reality TV show is going to change that."

"Good, because I don't know what I'd do without you."

"Right back at you, kiddo. I'm not going anywhere. You're stuck with me."

His words wrapped around her heart like a bear hug, making her feel like she was part of a family again. And in a way she was, her and Nick. And though she worried what Brad and the film crew would want them to do, she had a feeling this island adventure would only strengthen their friendship.

WE'LL ALWAYS BE FRIENDS. No stupid reality TV show is going to change that.

Three hours later, standing in waist deep water in a secluded cove with the film crew on a dinghy ten feet away, Nick believed the words whole-heartedly. But he wondered if the tiny scraps of blue fabric someone decided to call a bikini might change everything.

Sweat beaded on the back of his neck. If he liked seeing Addie in a swimsuit back in high school, he loved seeing her now.

Hot. Hot. Hot.

He wasn't talking air temperature.

She frolicked twenty feet from him, her breasts jiggling, her skin wet, her luscious curves barely covered. "Having fun?"

If he ignored the urge to tear the itty-bitty bikini off Addie and pretended the film crew didn't exist, he'd be having a blast. But she was all bubbly and smiles. No reason to ruin her fun. "Oh, yeah. How about you?"

She nodded, then pushed her wet hair off her face. She'd ditched her ponytail again. Good. He much preferred her hair worn loose, past her shoulders. "Being watched and filmed is creepy, but at least we aren't having to wear microphones."

Nick knew what she meant. The filming this morning had them paddleboarding to the cove while wearing microphones to capture their conversation. "Dunking wearing mikes would be dangerous."

She held up her arms as if to ward him off. "Please no dunking. There's not much to this swimsuit. One wrong move, and I'll be getting a fine from the FTC or need parts blacked out."

Come on, wrong move.

Crap. He shouldn't be thinking that.

Friendship was stronger than lust. Stronger than her swimsuit that might blow away with a strong gust of wind and leave her naked in the water. Stronger than her perfect C-cup breasts that he had no doubt would fit perfectly in his hand. Stronger than her bright-as-the-tropical-sun smile making him feel like he was the center of her universe.

"No worries." He raised his arms in surrender, more a reminder to himself than her. "I won't dunk you. Wouldn't want pics of my naked wife to go viral."

"Naked trophy wife." She stuck her tongue out at him.

He did the same. Man, she was sexy, even playing like a kid.

Wes jumped out of the dinghy with his camera leaving Dylan, the sound guy, and Conrad, the other cameraman, with Brad.

"Okay, Addie, move closer to Nick," Brad directed from the boat. "Splash him a few times."

Addie followed the instructions, wading through the water until she was five feet away, water dripping from her hair and down her soft skin. "Ready?" she asked Nick.

"You don't have to ask permission to splash me."

One shoulder lifted in a shrug. She sent a weak wave toward him.

Nick laughed. "You can splash harder than that."

"I'm trying to be nice."

"They haven't asked us to do much. If we perform now." He lowered his voice. "We might not have to later."

Her mouth formed a perfect *O*. "Good point."

"Show me what you've got."

Her splashes burned his eyes, but that wasn't going to stop him from getting his shots in.

"Your turn," he warned.

Addie opened her mouth to speak. Perfect target. He returned fire with a massive splash. A direct hit.

She coughed, wiped her face. "I'll get you for that, Mr. Cahill."

"I don't think you will, Mrs. Cahill or should that be, Mrs. Nice?"

"Mrs. Don't-Mess-With-Me."

She splashed him. He retaliated. The attack continued, water flying and laughter filling the air.

Over the years, distance had separated them physically, but never stopped them from staying in contact. They'd been through too much with his parents separating, reuniting, divorcing, and her grandfather's death when they were thirteen to not remain close. But spending time together now reminded him of their carefree and fun high school days. Happiness, pure and simple.

"Stop splashing and move closer together," Brad ordered.

So much for fun. Nick hoped this would be as easy as the rest of the morning.

Addie's smile tightened, her lips pressing together like a vice. No one else would notice, but Nick did and hated how uncomfortable she looked walking toward him, not quite a lamb to slaughter, but a close second. "Hey, honey, it's okay," he said softly.

She nodded once.

"When you're two feet closer, jump into Nick's arms and kiss him," Brad added. "Show us some serious lip-lock action."

Addie's eyes widened, her face a portrait in panic.

Aw, hell. This was what Nick thought would happen. He stopped walking. He'd grown up dreaming of kissing Addie, but never acted on those desires. Came close, but he hadn't wanted to scare her off or lose her friendship. He felt the same way now. Kissing for the hell of it was one thing. Being forced to kiss. No way.

Brad's blinding smile disappeared. "Got a problem, Nick?"

Yes. "No."

"You stopped walking. You're supposed to keep going toward Addie so you meet in the middle."

Nick shrugged.

"I thought green hats knew how to follow orders."

Every single muscle tensed. His jaw, too. "Berets. Green Berets."

"Just kidding."

He didn't say anything, though he flexed his fingers. Another joke and Brad would be searching for his veneers at the bottom of the dingy.

"Keep moving. Kissing your wife will be the easiest thing I ask of you today," Brad continued. "I'm sure you've done your fair share of womanizing over the years until you and Addie reconnected. Though you A-Team boys aren't as badass as Delta Force or SEALs. Those guys are real lady killers."

Nick balled his hands. He looked at Addie. "Thirty seconds is all I need. I promise I won't hurt him. Not too badly."

Something flashed in her eyes like a golden lightning bolt. She ran through the water, jumped into his arms, knocking him off his feet.

Nick fell back, cushioned by the water. His hands wrapped around her waist to keep her afloat. He regained his footing, but stayed low holding onto Addie. "Hey—"

"No hurting anyone." Her voice was low, but firm. "Understood?"

He opened his mouth to answer.

She kissed him hard on the lips.

What?

Whoa. A flame ignited low in his gut. This was unexpected. But wow.

Wow, wow, wow.

Her lips moved against his. Hands splayed his back, her fingers pressing into him with a sense of urgency.

Did he say wow?

Addie making the first move was a complete turn-on. The way she continued to kiss him . . . so hot. Nick couldn't believe this was happening, but he was going to make the most of opportunity.

His lips moved over hers, wanting more. She tasted salty and sweet like peanuts and chocolate. She smelled like that lotus scent and sunscreen, a potent combination making him lightheaded.

He didn't mind. Not one bit.

Her hunger and eagerness surprised him. No complaints. He'd dreamed of this moment as a randy teen and was not disappointed as a grown adult. His expectations had been exceeded. Ten . . . a hundred fold.

All he wanted was to keep kissing her.

A bird squawked. Waves rolled into them. The temperature seemed hotter than a few minutes before. A little heat wouldn't stop him. Not with a beautiful woman in his arms and her lips against his.

One kiss, another kiss, he lost track of the kisses and everything else. Not that he cared. His world was complete at the moment. Nothing else mattered, but Addie. Sweet

Addie.

Soft, smooth, wet skin pressed against him. His hands wanted to feel every inch of her. Addie didn't seem to mind so he touched her. Here, there, everywhere. He couldn't get enough of her.

She deepened the kiss. Her tongue explored, tangled, and danced with his.

Oh, yeah. Tingles shot across nerve endings. Pleasurable sensations pooled in his stomach, fueling the fire building inside. He burned with desire and heat.

More, he wanted more. He cupped her bottom, bringing her closer to him.

She wrapped her legs around him, running her fingers through her hair. She arched, pressing her hips against his.

His groin twitched, tightened. He knew what was coming next.

Crap. Nick jerked back, not getting far with her legs holding her to him.

Addie stared up, her lips parted like she wanted another kiss. He would be happy to oblige. No, he wouldn't. Couldn't.

Not with her.

Nick untangled her legs from him, made sure she was standing before he let go. He couldn't believe he'd gotten so turned-on by a simple kiss.

Nothing simple about her kiss, logic said matter-of-factly.

Shut up. Letting himself get carried away with Addie made him feel like a jerk. He hadn't been kissing a random woman he wanted to have sex with. He'd been kissing Addie. His friend, the one he was supposed to be looking out for, protecting. He'd failed. Big time.

Sure he'd had sex with other female friends, but Addie was different. She'd always been different from other girls ... women. Truth was, he needed her—her understanding, her compassion, her support, more than she needed him. That had always been the case with their friendship.

He couldn't screw up. Not with Addie.

But he'd come close.

So what if she kissed better than Nick imagined when he was younger? No reason to lose control and want to take her to bed. Hell, a few more minutes and he would have taken her right there, if she'd let him. He swore under this breath.

Addie wouldn't meet his gaze. Staring at the horizon, she bit her swollen lower lip, looking like she was ready to bolt. He didn't blame her for wanting to get away from him. Not after he'd responded to her kisses as if he'd been deployed and cut-off from women for months.

Calm down, Cahill. Figure out why this happened before you get your panties in a twist.

The words of his Team Sergeant, otherwise known as "Team Daddy," sounded in Nick's head. The voice had been second only to God on his ODA team. You listened and followed directions, which was what Nick would do now.

A list of why he might have acted the way formed in his mind—strong physical chemistry, attraction pushed aside for too long, not having sex to show his boss he wasn't a player. Yeah, Nick could explain his reaction to Addie's kiss. He glanced up at the blue sky and saluted. *Thanks, Team Daddy.*

"Cut." Brad clapped his hand. "You two are naturals."

Damn. The film crew. Nick had forgotten about them, but his main concern was making sure Addie was okay. "Do you guys need anything else?"

"We're good," Brad said, over the sound of the engine igniting. "Enjoy your lunch. It's waiting for you on the beach. Make the most of the cove, then paddleboard back to the resort. We'll see you this afternoon."

They picked up Wes, then the boat motored away.

"Good riddance." Nick looked at Addie, who was jogging through the water toward the beach.

Nick followed. He would downplay the kiss, especially his reaction, and focus on them successfully pulling off being honeymooners, even though he had forgotten about the crew and cameras being there.

But she didn't need to know that.

And wouldn't.

Chapter Five

*O*H, *NO. SHE'D kissed Nick. Kissed him so many times she'd lost track. Worse, she'd been all over him. Literally.*

Addie's feet hit the sand. She wanted to run except she hadn't a clue where to go. Beyond the sand were palm trees and greenery. This was a secluded cove, reachable only by water, no path to the resort. That meant she was stuck here on a sigh-worthy beach with the gorgeous guy who'd nearly kissed her out of her bikini. Worse, she wouldn't have minded. Physical awareness of him buzzed through her body.

So. Not. Good.

She plopped down on the blanket the resort had laid out for a picnic. A canopy of ivory fabric provided shade. A champagne bottle chilled in a silver bucket.

Better not drink too much. Nick's kisses made her tipsy enough. Though chugging champagne might be a way for her to forget about what she'd done, captured on film, for all to see.

Any normal woman would have kissed Nick, maybe twirled a lock of his hair with her finger, and rubbed his back, not gone after him with reckless, wanton desire, complete with tongue action and legs wrapped around him. Her cheeks burned.

What had she been thinking?

She hadn't been. That was the problem. She'd given into the moment, into stupid teenage fantasies of kissing Nick, without a thought to what she was doing as a woman being filmed for a reality TV show.

Stupid. Stupid. Stupid.

The worst part? She had no idea what she was going to say to Nick. Her friend. Her *platonic* friend.

Was there any chance of a volcano erupting nearby? She'd happily sacrifice herself because that was the only way she could save face.

"Addie," Nick yelled from the water.

She didn't look his way. She . . . couldn't.

Not with her heart pounding, her breathing ragged, and her face heated, likely the shade of a hothouse tomato. The way he'd touched her had sent explosions through her. She hadn't wanted to stop. A part of her wished they hadn't.

Lust or temporary insanity? Maybe a combination.

"Hey." Nick emerged from the sea like Poseidon himself, water streaming down his athletic body, over muscles, tattoos, and gleaming skin, making her mouth go dry. The gold band on his finger shone, mocking her reaction to his kisses and reminding her, like their marriage, whatever happened between them wasn't real. "Hungry?"

"Yes." As long as more of his tasty kisses weren't on the menu. Another one might push her over the edge or make her want to get naked. She rubbed her aching forehead. Maybe the sun was affecting her brain and common sense.

"Me, too." He shook his arms, sending droplets of water spraying, then sat next to her on the blanket. His smile wasn't forced, no lines of worry around his mouth or forehead. He looked the same, as always. Of course, kisses were no big deal to Nick. They were a regular part of his life followed by sex.

Unlike her.

She imagined the neon-colored words "Take Me Now" stamped on her forehead and glowing brightly. All due to a few kisses. Hot ones, but still . . .

Pathetic.

Burying her head in the sand might be a more achievable option than finding a volcano.

"Being in the water for a long time is hard work after paddleboarding. You get tired and work up an appetite." He reached for the picnic basket. "Let's see what's for lunch."

Oh, Nick. Her heart melted. He wasn't going to bring up the kiss or anything else. Of course not. He avoided any kind of confrontation, always had. But they had nine days of acting like honeymooners ahead of them. They couldn't avoid this conversation, not if she wanted to remain sane.

Addie needed to say something, apologize for attacking him the way she had. Oh, she had a reason to kiss him the way she had. Nick had looked so . . . intense. A wild, almost maniacal expression had crossed his face and his eyes hardened like stone. She hadn't been scared of him, but she'd been frightened by what he might do to Brad and been spurred to act. But she had to take responsibility for what she'd done and her response to the kisses. "We need to talk."

His jaw tensed. "Shoot."

Addie took a breath, then another, mustering her courage. Okay, she could do this.

"I'm sorry for jumping on top of you and kissing you the way I did. I didn't mean . . ." The words rushed from her mouth like soda from a shaken can, spewing every which way. "I thought you were going to hurt Brad. I figured if I distracted you—"

"I would forget what Brad said."

She nodded. "I debated between kissing you and dropping my bikini top. Kissing was faster."

"It worked." Nick winked. "Though the bikini top would have, too."

He wasn't upset. Good. Maybe she shouldn't be. People kissed all the time. Well, everyone except her. Not passionately, at least. Not for a long time, but no reason to freak out now. If anyone understood her, Nick did.

"The crew seemed pleased by our enthusiasm," he added.

Nodding, she stared at a tiny sand crab digging a hole in the sand. As soon as her lips touched Nick's, she'd forgotten about the filming. No cameras and crew had existed. Only

Nick. Getting caught up in her first real—well, pretend—passionate kiss in years could happen to anyone when your toes curled, right? She looked over at him. "No retakes required."

"We got it right the first time." His grin spread to his eyes, crinkling the corners. He was so gorgeous. "Thanks to you, Brad got the lip action he wanted."

"A little awkward." There. She'd said what else was bothering her.

"You think?"

Huh? She searched Nick's face to see if he was joking. He looked serious. Odd, because friends normally didn't straddle friends while wearing almost nothing and kissing them at the same time. "Didn't you?"

"Seemed like a regular kiss to me."

"Oh." She didn't know what to say. Not many kisses had left her clinging to a guy, hot and aching for more. But then again, kissing wasn't something she'd done since she dropped out of college. "It's just, we're friends. Things have always been platonic between us, and then we're out in the water kissing like crazy."

"Not awkward. We did what they asked us to do. We kissed like two newlyweds who can't keep their hands off each other. The film crew is happy. Brad, especially." Nick opened the lid to the picnic basket. "If I didn't know better, I'd think we were on our honeymoon."

Her heart hammered against her breastbone, so loudly

she could count each beat. She felt the same way. Maybe that was why she'd felt so awkward. Kissing Nick seemed natural and right, the way she'd dreamed kissing him would feel. Her desire hadn't been faked. Nothing about her actions had been pretend. "Then I . . . we succeeded."

He nodded, removing containers from the basket. "I have no doubt we're going to pull this off now."

Addie couldn't disagree, but this felt weird. Friends shouldn't be so comfortable kissing one another.

"We've got lobster, roasted vegetables, bread, fresh fruit, and cookies for lunch," he said.

"I know what I'm starting with." Exotic orange, yellow, and pink fruit filled a small basket he'd set out. She chose a red apple, something familiar, and took a bite.

Kissing Nick had proven they could act like a honeymoon couple. Nothing else had changed. But a part of Addie felt like everything in her life had done a one-eighty because of the kiss. She couldn't stop thinking about how being in Nick's arms felt or how his kiss tasted or how she wanted . . . more.

"What?" he said.

"Huh?"

"You keep biting your lip."

"Do not," she countered. "I'm eating an apple."

"You're doing it now."

She realized she was gnawing on her lip.

"Tell me what's on your mind," he said.

Addie took another bite.

Nick pulled out the champagne. Water from the ice dripped down the bottle. "Come on. We've talked about almost everything. This isn't any different."

True, but . . . "Two subjects have been off limits."

"Only one after you loaned me a backpack filled with tampons and pads."

"I forgot about that."

"I haven't. Especially since I wasn't the one to find them. Mickey Henry had that honor. Man, the look on his face." Nick laughed. "As long as you don't want to talk about having sex with some guy, I'm good."

What about wanting to have sex with him? She shook the thought from her head. "The kiss seemed almost . . ."

"What?"

"Too easy."

A look of relief flashed across his face. "Easy, yes. But explainable if you take a look around."

She did. "A secluded cove?"

He nodded. "We're in a tropical cove with clear turquoise water and fine, white sand. Palm trees lining the edges. Rugged rocks to provide additional privacy."

"I can see why the crew wanted to film here today."

"Exactly. The entire place, this island, screams romance. That's why couples come from all over the world to vacation here." He opened the champagne bottle. The cork popped. "The setting adds oomph to kisses."

She saw his point, except—"Even kisses between friends?"

"Especially those. Look at us. We're not wearing cold-weather gear. Lots of skin-to-skin contact. Easy to get caught up in the moment."

She straightened. "Were you caught up, too?"

"Damn straight. Couldn't you tell?"

His hands had been all over her. She swallowed. "I wasn't analyzing what was happening as we kissed."

"Me, either. Which is another reason the kiss was so easy. We weren't thinking." He poured champagne into two glasses, then handed her one. "The others shouldn't be much different."

Others? A shiver ran down her spine. Addie drank from her champagne glass. Too much. She choked. Coughed.

Nick touched her back. "You okay?"

Her eyes watered. She nodded.

He handed her a water bottle. "This might help."

She took a drink of water, then wiped her mouth with the back of her hand. "Thanks. Guess that completes this morning's freak-out."

He touched her arm, gently, as if she were something special, and a longing to be that to him sparked inside her. "You're doing great. We can handle whatever they throw at us."

She waited for him to remove his hand. He didn't. Nor did she mind. Heat emanated from his fingertips against her skin. That felt different from his touches during the kissing, but nice, too. "I hope so."

"We've got this."

If only his confidence was contagious. Addie would have to see how they did the next time. But no matter what she might be feeling, however good or right or natural kissing and touching him might seem, none of this was real. Not their marriage. Not the honeymoon. Not any kisses.

She stared at his hand still touching her.

Addie couldn't forget anything with Nick other than friendship was nothing more than a fantasy. One she didn't dare to dream would come true.

"I DIDN'T THINK anything could beat this morning in the cove, but this comes close." Four hours later, Nick lay face down on a massage table, a white sheet covering him, fresh flowers strewn about and the smell of coconut oil in the air. Swaying palm fronds and crashing waves provided the background music. "I guess Brad's not so bad."

"Pina Coladas on the beach when we arrived back followed by a couple's massage. Only fifteen minutes of filming. I'd say he's a good guy." Addie was on a table an arm's reach away. "Aren't you glad you didn't punch him?"

"Yes." Though Nick's body felt as if he'd stepped out of a MMA ring without landing a hit. Kissing, talking about kissing, trying to pretend he wasn't looking forward to any more fake kisses while sharing a romantic lobster lunch with butter dripping from the corner of her mouth had knotted him worse than a bag of unspooled paracord. No easy way to untangle his muscles. But thanks to the expert masseuse, each swirl of her hands evaporated some of the tension. "This could be his way of making sure I don't hit him later."

"Not that you would."

"You said no violence. I'll be good." Oh, man. The masseuse performed some sort of percussion move on his back. "I'm feeling very good. Massages sure don't suck."

She laughed. "I see more of these in our future."

"Now, you're talking."

Addie didn't sound wigged out anymore. That made him happy. Though he couldn't take credit. The champagne and cocktails were helping. The massage, too. Though a dip in the water and paddleboarding hadn't hurt.

She lay on her stomach. The sheet pushed down to her waist, exposing her back. Her face was pressed through the cutout, her hair spread over the top part of the table. The masseuse ran her hands over Addie's glistening back.

Sexy, but . . .

This wasn't the time to be admiring her smooth skin or anything else. He looked through the hole in the table at the floor. They were friends. Friends who found themselves in an unusual circumstance. Friends who got caught up in kissing each other this morning. But still friends, platonic friends.

Staring at her, admiring her, being attracted to her, was not a smart move when he wanted to do was reach out and rub her back. He had to watch himself around her, especially during kisses.

Addie sighed. The pleasure-filled sound sent a burst of heat rushing through him. Or maybe that was due to whatever the masseuse was doing to his spine. Releasing toxins or chakras or whatever woo-woo term was in use these days.

Yeah, that had to be it. Not Addie, something else. "So when do you want to schedule our next massage?"

"Tomorrow."

"There could be a waiting list."

"I hope not." She took a breath, then exhaled slowly. "Talk about magic fingers. This feels like we've won a prize in addition to the grand prize."

"The cherry on top."

"Don't forget the whip cream."

Oh, baby, the things they could do to each other with whipped cream . . .

If they were a real couple.

Which they weren't.

Dammit.

He counted the lines in the bamboo floor hoping to bring his temperature back to room level and erasing the playful, sexy, and messy images in his mind. This vacation was going to test the limits of his self-control in more than one way.

Whether this would be good or not, he couldn't tell. He wouldn't know until he and Addie were back in San Diego where they only had to deal with a fake marriage, not the honeymoon and reality TV stuff.

Another sigh escaped from Addie. "I wish we could stay here forever."

Yeah, Nick knew how she felt. But he couldn't get lost in the tropical fantasy if he wanted to stay in control. "Paradise might lose its appeal."

"Never."

She sounded relaxed and sleepy. The way he felt. "Let's see how you sound after a nap this afternoon."

"I'm not changing my mind." She yawned. "Though a nap sounds heavenly. If I can stay awake now."

He looked over, reached across the space between their tables and touched her forearm. Her skin was soft and smooth beneath his calloused fingertips. "Close your eyes. If you fall asleep no one will care. You deserve this."

Her gaze met his. Her eyes were slightly dilated, her lids heavy. Beautiful. "Only if you do the same. You deserve this, too."

Nick closed his eyes. An image of Addie appeared, one with a satisfied smile and happy, twinkling eyes. She wore a white dress similar to the one she'd worn at their wedding, but this time had a veil on her head and bouquet of pink flowers in her hands.

A ball of warmth, comfortable and complete, settled around his heart. His eyes sprang open.

What the hell was going on? His daydreams—hell, his thoughts—ran more the line of a naked hot chick with huge breasts and a round, firm butt.

Brides were his worst nightmare since Carrie. Handing over his paychecks like a lovesick fool, making plans for spending his life with her, keeping a list of baby names for his son or daughter, only to return home to see her waiting for him with his engagement ring on her finger and a baby bump too small for the kid to be his. He closed his eyes, pushing away the bad memories. He'd gotten over the betrayal and hurt, but he was not going to be played again. He was never getting married. Not for real anyway. Imagining Addie as a bride should not be happening.

He must be more tired than he realized. Exhausted.

A nap would clear the insane image from his mind. Nick closed his eyes. At least he hoped so.

ADDIE STRETCHED OUT on the patio's daybed, rested, following a nap back at the *bure*. The massage had relieved her stress and loosened her muscles, making her think she could get through the other eight days. But after hearing from Emily, Addie wasn't so sure. She adjusted the belt of the robe she wore over her blue bikini.

A snore sounded. Nick. He slept on the hammock. She'd

never heard him snore. Not on the plane or last night. Maybe she hadn't noticed or maybe he was that tired.

Addie glanced at the cell phone next to her. What was taking Emily so long to reply?

The Snapchat app, popular with teens, was new to Addie, and the only one Emily would use to answer questions about the honeymoon contest. After reading the posts so far, Addie understood why her friend would want the words to disappear.

She used her straw to poke at the sliced cucumbers, limes, and mint leaves floating in her water glass, then took a sip.

Wait until Nick found out the truth. A good thing he'd promised no violence or Emily would be a goner. Not really, but given the unease Addie felt, he was not going to be happy.

Nick stretched his arms over his head. His gaze met hers. She stared transfixed, as if connected to him by an imaginary string or cable. He didn't say anything, but words didn't seem necessary.

This was how they'd been in high school, but here the connection felt . . . different. Stronger, stirring a desire she'd never felt before. Strange given the amount of time they'd spent together then compared to now. Maybe this romantic setting was messing with her mind, making her want something she could never have.

A reply arrived from Emily. A stealthily taken picture of

her boss followed by the words, "Gotta go."

"Who was that?" Nick asked.

"Emily."

"She's been ignoring my texts. What did she say about the contest?"

Addie stared at her cell phone. The conversation was over. Messages would soon disappear.

"That bad," Nick said.

"Depends on how you look at it."

He hopped out of the hammock and joined her on the day bed. "Any chance of us getting arrested?"

"No."

"Then I'm good." He bent his elbow and rested his head on his hand. "So . . ."

"The honeymoon giveaway was a way to find a couple for the reality TV show so competitors wouldn't know what kind of show the network was planning."

"Emily couldn't know this."

"The network is one of her ad agency's biggest clients. She's on the account."

Nick made a face. "This entire thing was fixed from the beginning."

"No, they planned on using the real contest winners, but none of the entries appealed to the agency or production company. Too down home. Too urban. Too many piercings. The list went on and on. One person at the agency was fired. That's when Emily was told to find a couple or else."

Nick pointed to Addie's water. "Mind if I have a sip?"

"Go ahead. Mama Lani made a pitcher of the stuff. It's in the fridge."

He drank. "So if Emily hadn't found the right couple, she could have been fired."

"Explains her excitement when we got engaged."

"She kept her job by selling us out."

Addie understood his harsh tone, but they hadn't been sent to a swampy, mosquito-infested place. "We're not exactly slumming it. Emily sent us on a luxurious free vacation and picked out our new wardrobes."

"She has style and taste, but she used us to save her job."

"You got married for your job."

"That's different."

"Pot and kettle."

"Not really."

"Same thing. Emily apologized for not telling the truth, but she didn't think we'd go if we knew about the reality TV show."

"Damn straight we wouldn't have come," Nick said. "Forgot buying her a souvenir. She can take us to brunch at the Del when we get back."

"No. In case you forgot, we're lying to her about our marriage. If the truth comes out, she'll be fired. Her job is her life. She'd be devastated."

"So now two jobs are on the line with this marriage sham." He half-laughed. "Unbelievable."

"At least we know how we ended up on Starfish Island."

"Yeah, and I'm glad you made us an appointment for another massage." He rubbed the back of his neck. "My muscles are tightening again."

Addie's first instinct was to offer help. But her hands on his skin would not be a smart move. Random thoughts about Nick and her together kept popping up, but she needed to remember he might be her husband, but he wasn't her Prince Charming. No matter how amazing his kisses made her feel. "I'll see if I can get the appointment time moved up."

Chapter Six

THE NEXT FEW days, Nick fell into a comfortable rhythm each morning with a run followed by a swim. The exercise kept him in shape and let him burn off energy. He wasn't used to relaxing for this long or pretending to be a husband. Nick didn't mind, either. That surprised him. But hanging with Addie filled him with contentment, a way he hadn't felt in a long time, so long he couldn't remember when. Maybe he'd found the key to a happy marriage his parents had missed—marry your best friend and don't have sex.

On the patio, he rinsed off the sand from his legs. A quick shower inside, a change of clothes, and he'd be ready for breakfast once Addie woke. After that, the work would begin.

Not really.

Playing "in love" honeymooners wasn't a tough gig. He couldn't believe they'd planned to go their separate ways during the honeymoon. That wouldn't have been fun.

Spending time with Addie was the best part.

Kissing Addie was his second favorite. Who cared if the kisses were for the camera? A kiss was a kiss, and she was a great kisser. He kept reminding himself not to get carried away again. Emotions were easier to push aside than the physical stuff.

He walked into the *bure* taking soft steps. After years of getting up at the crack of dawn, Addie preferred waking without an alarm clock. She'd also ditched wearing shoes and ponytails unless she needed her hair out of the way for an activity. All steps in the right direction.

Island life agreed with her. Her tired eyes and stress had disappeared. The weight she'd been carrying had lifted. She looked happier, more beautiful, without the baggage of the past dragging her down.

Nick glanced at the bed. Empty. "Addie?"

"Bula, bula, Mr. Nick." Out on the patio, Mama Lani poked her head inside the *bure*. She carried an overflowing tray of food along with glasses of juices and two tall mugs with straws sticking out, most likely smoothies. "Your wife is in the bathroom. She woke up early. So excited to go snorkeling you'd think she'd never seen the ocean before. Reminds me of one of my grandbabies."

Nick joined their mama *bure* outside. "Addie's re-experiencing many things during this trip."

Him, too. The feelings for her he'd buried back in high school kept coming back. But he wasn't about to risk their friendship for something fleeting. All he had to do was hold on and stay in control until they returned to San Diego. His upcoming job assignments would give them some distance and let their friendship return to normal.

"Addie told me about her grandmother and what happened with the cottage." Mama Lani set the table. "Such a shame family would do that to their own."

"Greed makes people do strange things." As if he were one to talk. He'd married a friend to keep his job. Maybe Emily and he had both sold out Addie for a paycheck. The realization didn't sit well, though he knew she was getting something from the marriage, too. "But you can't live without money."

"The key is figuring out how much money you need. More isn't always better."

"Life is simple on Starfish Island."

"Life is only complicated if you make it so."

"I like simple." Which was why being friends with Addie made the most sense even if her kisses set him on fire.

"Then live simply. Do work that satisfies you. Earn what you need. Enjoy what you have."

"Then you'll be happy," he added.

Mama Lani's gaze narrowed. "Happiness is a choice, Mr. Nick. Anyone who says otherwise is a fool."

He had a feeling the woman thought he was a fool. That bothered him because Addie valued Mama Lani's opinion. "I'll be sure to choose happy. Easy to do with Addie around."

"Take lessons from your bride. Addie is young, like you, but when you look in her eyes, you can see she's an old soul."

"She was always different." He remembered when his mom had left the first time. Addie had found him at the playground and held his hand while he cried. She did the same thing when his mother returned and his father took off. "Even when we were five."

"Is that why you proposed in kindergarten?" Mama Lani teased.

He hadn't been able to imagine Addie not being in his life. She'd been a little girl but she was also the one constant in his unstable life. If he could have moved in with her and her grandparents, he would have. "Addie has always been a catch."

"I have no doubt." The amusement in Mama Lani's voice matched the look in her eyes. "You were a smart young man to realize that."

He straightened, pleased to receive a compliment from Addie's new favorite person. "Thank you."

"Nick!" Addie yelled from inside.

"On the patio."

Footsteps drew nearer. "Close your eyes."

He did.

"What color do you think we're wearing today?" she asked.

"Black."

"Nope."

"Not purple."

"No."

He liked the playful tone in her voice. "Can you give me a hint?"

"I'm wearing my favorite color."

Pink. He swore under his breath. That was a step up from purple, but several rungs down from red or orange. "Please don't tell me you're wearing pink."

"Okay, I won't tell you, but you can open your eyes." Addie fun pose in her bikini showed off her long legs and toned body. "Ta-da. Hot pink."

Sexy. Healthy. Her skin had turned a honeyed color in spite of the sunscreen she'd been applying and the wide-brimmed straw hat she wore.

"You look amazing," he said.

"You're going to look hot in your swim trunks."

Nick made a face.

"Hot pink isn't so bad," she said. "There's a band of white around the waistband."

"Well, that changes everything."

"Not," they said at the same time, then laughed.

"Jinx." Addie pointed at him. "You owe me a Coke."

"You don't drink sodas."

"Then you owe me a cosmopolitan. I think I'll have a pink one. Not until later, of course."

"Of course." He noticed Mama Lana setting out the food. "Guess I'll have to take one for the team and put on the hot pink."

She grinned. "You're the best fr . . . husband."

Panic flashed on her face. She'd nearly slipped up with Mama Lani here, but Addie had caught herself.

"Don't forget it." He walked passed her, snagging a quick kiss. "But when you're shopping for my birthday, Christmas, or anniversary presents, think manly colors."

"Manly, huh?"

"Black, brown, navy blue, camo. Got my reputation to uphold." He winked. "I'm going to shower, then I'll be right back. Unless you care to join me?"

Addie's face paled, his first clue he'd put her in a tough spot. Not intentionally. Crap. The words had slipped from his lips without much thought. Acting like husband and wife was becoming second nature, even when the cameras weren't around.

Her wide-eyed gaze bounced from him to Mama Lani. "I . . ."

"Kidding." Another wink he hoped would make up for his lapse. "You've showered and need to eat. Long day ahead."

She nodded with a look of relief. "I am hungry."

He was, too. For her.

Not the right response, but hard to feel otherwise. The bikini, he told himself, except he'd been staring at her gorgeous face and the smattering of freckles. "Save me some food."

"Will do." Addie's lips slanted in a wry grin. "I'll take a rain check on that shower, okay?"

Nick swallowed around a mango-sized lump in his throat. He knew she wasn't serious, but a part of him wished she were. "Sounds perfect."

Much better than the cold shower he would be taking this morning.

OUT IN THE water that afternoon, Addie kicked her fins to keep up with Nick, who followed a school of bright green and yellow fish headed toward a colorful reef. She stared through her mask amazed at the world underneath the water. Snorkeling was becoming her favorite activity on the island. Next to kissing Nick.

For the camera only, of course.

But honestly, she had a good time with him no matter what they did. He was nothing but fun and games today, suggesting a challenge as they left the *bure* this morning. He wanted to see if they could outlast the film crew in the water. Unbeknownst to Brad and company. She'd agreed.

Game on.

Now her skin wrinkled from being in the water so long, but the amazing sights she'd snorkeling had been worth feeling waterlogged.

Wes, decked out in full scuba gear, swam below them filming. Bubbles rose from his regulator but his tank had to be getting low on air. He and Conrad, filming from the dinghy, had switched positions once.

Addie held Nick's hand, their fingers laced together, as if they should always be that way, in the water or out. He gave a tug, then pointed with his other hand. A blue fish circling a red and orange plant a short distance away.

She nodded, noticing a burst of air bubbles rather than a steady stream from Wes. A sigh, perhaps?

Wes motioned to his air gage, then waved.

Yay! They'd outlasted the crew. Well, Wes. With a smile, Addie kicked toward the little fish Nick had pointed out.

She stared through her goggles at the fish, who stared back at her. The fish darted around the plant, then disappeared. Guess he didn't want company.

Ready for a breath of air without the snorkel, she raised her head out of the water, pushed the goggles on top of her head and cleared the wet hair plastered against her face.

Nick joined her on the surface. His mask came up. The snorkel hung at the edge of his mouth. He hugged her. "A win for Team Cahill."

"We work well together." The victory hug felt pretty darn good, but then again, she enjoyed every minute and activity with Nick. "Now let's call it quits. We've been in the water so long my wrinkles have wrinkles. And I'm thirsty."

"Cosmopolitan time or another frou-frou umbrella drink?" he asked.

She raised her chin. "I happen to like umbrellas. I'll be

taking a collection home with me."

"A good thing I'll have room in my bag."

The film crew's dinghy motored toward them, cameras pointed their way.

Nick cursed. "They're still filming us."

Addie sighed. "So much for beating them."

"Guess they want the money shot." That was what Nick called their kisses. "How does short and sweet sound?"

"Good." They'd named their kisses while floating on a raft for two and being brought an endless supply of Piña Coladas. Tried and true. Short and sweet. Passionate and prolonged. Long and lustful. Hungry and hot. Explosive and everlasting. Not that she could describe the differences between anyone of them, except short and sweet. That one she could handle, even if she longed for more. Addie wiped the water from her face. "Hard to do anything else while treading water wearing snorkel gear."

The boat came closer.

"Ready?" Nick asked, his arms around her.

No, but she nodded anyway. "Showtime."

Addie kissed him. Her mouth moved gently over his, the taste of salt and water and heat on his lips. She loved how he tasted, how he felt.

He tightened his arms around her, pressing his mouth against hers.

Sensations pulsated through her. She reminded herself to kick so Nick wasn't holding them both up.

"I've got you," he murmured.

He sure had. Addie would never get enough of his kisses. She clung to him, opening her mouth wider and deepening the kiss. He followed her lead, pulling her closer, until she felt his heartbeat against her breast.

Heat built within her. A growing ache, too. Need.

A warning bell sounded in her head.

Short and sweet.

Oops. She kissed him once more, then pulled back, expecting him to let go of her. He didn't.

His charming smile made her want to kiss him again. But she knew that wasn't necessary. The film crew had what the needed. Unlike her. She wanted . . .

Don't go there.

Nothing more was possible.

Nick grinned. "That was more hungry and hot, than short and sweet."

"You complaining?"

"Not at all." His mouth slanted. "Looks like they got their money shot and are finished."

Her lips throbbed from his kiss. She forced herself not to touch them. "I'm finished, too."

"It's been a long day."

"I'm ready to go back to the *bure* and rest."

"A nap is in order. Don't forget. We're having dinner at the resort, then drinks at the bar. Time to mingle and meet other guests."

"Bored with me?" she joked, though she wouldn't blame him if he were. Sleeping and shower time was the only times they hadn't been together since they arrived on the island five days ago. "I won't be offended if you are."

"Nope." His arms slid from around her, making her miss his warmth. "But if we tell the crew we're having another private dinner, they're going to want to film us."

"Good point," Addie agreed. She enjoyed their dinners alone, but not having to deal with the film crew while she ate would be a relief. "Getting out and socializing with the other guests will be fun."

HOURS LATER, SHE stood at the bar next to Nick, wishing they'd eaten alone and were being filmed by the crew. Oh, she'd been having fun until five minutes ago when a beautiful, busty strawberry blonde woman in a low-cut blouse sat at the opposite end of the bar. Addie might have been out of the dating scene for a while, but she recognized the I-want-you signals being sent Nick's way. She couldn't believe the nerve of the woman.

Who flirted so blatantly with a guy's wife next to him?

Addie's blood pressure spiraled. She fought the urge to flash her wedding band and kiss Nick on the lips. Territorial, yes, but the need to stake her claim was strong, even if she had no more right to him than the flirtatious stranger.

Nick didn't seem to notice the attention, but everyone

else, including the staff, was staring at her. Maybe Nick was ignoring the woman or pretending not to see her. They were getting good at playacting, the line between real and fantasy sometimes blurred, but Addie hadn't forgotten their agreement. Discrete affairs were okay. A reasonable request given this was going to be a five-year marriage of convenience.

So why did the woman's blatant interest in Nick make Addie so uncomfortable and a little sick to her stomach?

Maybe she thought he'd take a break from flirting around during their honeymoon. Maybe she needed more food—a get-her-through-this chocolate something or other.

Addie touched his shoulder. "I'm going to see if any chocolate mousse is left."

He picked up his beer. "I'll come with you."

She wanted him with her, more than anything, but this was part of their arrangement, for better or worse. Putting off the inevitable would only make dealing with women flirting and wanting to pursue Nick harder the next time. "Stay here and finish your beer."

His forehead creased. "You sure?"

"I'm sure." Well, sort of. She was curious to see if he flirted back.

He smiled at her. "Enjoy the dessert."

Addie nodded again. She shouldn't be upset or disturbed or anything. Yet she was.

She walked to the outdoor dining area, took a bowl of chocolate mousse from the dessert display, then sat at a table with a direct view of the bar where she could see Nick. Well, his backside. She kind of understood why a moth might dive-bomb a tiki torch. She couldn't look away.

Before she stuck her spoon into the dessert, the strawberry blonde sidled up to Nick. She held a drink in one hand and touched his shoulder with the other.

Not wasting any time.

Addie shoved a spoonful of mousse into her mouth. The whipped chocolate went down smoothly, but she could be eating white rice for all she tasted.

Nick chatted with the woman. Addie could only see the backs of heads, but she imagined they were smiling, especially the woman. Addie stabbed her spoon into the mousse.

The woman flipped her hair behind her shoulder with a practiced flair, the kind reserved for actresses, supermodels, and socialites. Nick laughed. The woman pressed her chest against his upper arm. He didn't move away, but downed the rest of his beer as if he wanted to get out of there.

Reality smacked Addie in the stomach. This didn't look like flirting but wanting to fool around. She covered her mouth with her hand.

Darn him. Couldn't he have waited until they were off the island? If he got caught, he would blow their happy couple cover. Would Nick think sex with a stranger was worth his job and Emily's?

Yes.

The Nick that Addie had known most of her life was a

lady's man, player, heartbreaker. But here on the island, she'd forgotten. Forgotten about his dating habits. Forgotten about his reputation. Forgotten about women's response to his good looks and charm.

She shouldn't expect Nick to act differently. That went against his nature, but watching him now felt strange, almost . . . wrong. She didn't understand why.

Back in high school, when Nick had asked out one of her friends, Addie had told herself being his long-term friend was more important than being his short-term date. When he was deployed, she'd understood and supported him when he proposed to Carrie, knowing his baby needed a father. But Addie couldn't rationalize why she wanted to dump her bowl of mousse on the woman's head. Or why Nick needed to do this *now*?

When Addie wanted him sleeping with . . .

Well, not with another woman.

The bartender placed a cocktail and another beer bottle in front of Nick and the woman. The strawberry blonde raised her glass in a toast, the way Addie had done with Nick on the airplane and their first dinner. The mousse hardened in her stomach like a leaden weight.

Okay, she didn't expect Nick to be celibate for the next five years, but she hadn't imagined feeling so conflicted over seeing him with another woman. And tonight was only the beginning.

Could she handle this for the next five years? Did she

have a choice?

Addie had no idea, but she couldn't watch any longer. She stood, then headed for a path that didn't go past the bar.

Not that Nick would notice she'd left. He hadn't glanced at her once. He was too preoccupied and enthralled with the woman to care about Addie.

And his not caring hurt more than she ever imagined.

NICK TOOK A swig of his beer. The woman named Chantal pressed her hip against his thigh. She bent to give him a better view of her breasts through her low-cut top. Sexy, but the executive assistant, on the island to attend a wedding, needed a lesson in subtlety.

"I went on a long hike today." The your-place-or-mine gleam in her eyes suggested she would be open to whatever he wanted tonight. "My muscles are so sore."

A week ago—hell, five days ago—he would have been all over Chantal, flattered by her interest and eager to see how far he could take this. Pretty far, given her touches and body language.

But tonight her attention annoyed him. He wasn't interested in getting hit on or making any moves. The bartender had brought over another round of drinks when he finished his beer. Two sips and Nick was ready to get out of here. He'd seen Addie's reflection in the glass artwork above the bar. He wished she would finish her dessert, come back and save him from Chantal. But he seemed to be on his own. "Those hikes can be tough."

"Mmmm-hmmm. A back rub would be heavenly." Chantal leaned closer, her breath warm against his ear. "How about you come to my *bure* and help me feel better?"

Talk about easy. None of the film crew was around to follow him. Nick could avoid being seen by the resort staff. He had Addie's permission to do what he wanted. Nothing stood in the way of his having a night of hot sex in the tropics.

Except he didn't feel like doing that.

Nick took a long pull from his bottle. The beer felt cool down his throat.

Why was he being so good tonight? Not his usual MO.

The gold band on his finger shone beneath the lights hanging from the bar. Years ago, Addie's grandmother had told him the wedding rings symbolized a union—a lifetime of love with no end. He'd been a teenager, but had never forgotten her words, because they were the antithesis of his parents' marriage. He'd thought of the words when he ordered an engagement ring for Carrie over the Internet. He'd remembered the words when he was buying two gold bands for him and Addie.

"What do you say?" Chantal's tone sounded hopeful. "Ready to go?"

What the hell was he doing here with this woman instead of Addie?

"No." The word was sharp and decisive, but he wanted Chantal to know he was serious. Real marriage or fake one, he wasn't going to fool around on his honeymoon. Addie deserved better. He set his beer on the bar. "I'm married."

"I know, but you're so hot I don't mind." Chantal fluttered her eyelashes. "No one will find out."

"Doesn't matter." Sex wasn't part of his and Addie's marriage arrangement, but he wanted to spend time with her, no one else. "I'd know."

Chantal pouted. "But—"

"Not happening." Nick glanced up at a metallic sculpture hanging above the bar. The reflection showed Addie's dessert bowl on the table, but she wasn't there. He turned. No sign of her. Crap. His pulse kicked up. He stood. "I need to find my wife."

Chantal's mouth formed a perfect *O*, as if she wasn't used to be turning down by any man.

Why had Addie left? He went to the table where she'd been eating her dessert. The spot provided a direct line of sight to where he'd sat with Chantal.

Nick cursed. He didn't know what Addie had seen or misinterpreted, but he needed to find her.

He checked the bar area in case she'd returned. He asked the staff, but none had seen Addie leave. He would make a quick pass along the beach to check if she'd gone on a walk, then go to the *bure*.

Waves rolled to shore. A couple walked arm-in-arm

along the sand. No Addie. Nick noticed someone sitting at the end of the dock. The flickering torches cast too many shadows to tell who was there, but he recognized the long hair—Addie.

Relief slowed his pulse and breathing. Tension, however, continued to bunch his muscles.

Nick walked toward the end of the dock. He had a feeling he'd screwed up, at least in Addie's mind, and wasn't sure what to say. His parents' had given him a distorted view of so-called committed couples. He'd never been a good boyfriend. His attempt at being a fiancé had failed miserably. But he wanted to do better, be better, with Addie.

The moon hung low in the dark sky. Waves hit the dock. Lanterns and torches lit the area with a warm glow.

Addie sat at the end of the dock, her feet in the water. He did the same. "Why'd you take off?"

She drew a circle in the water with her big toe. "Figured you wanted to hang with new people tonight."

"I want to be with you."

She glanced over her shoulder at the resort. "But that woman at the bar who was talking to you—"

"Not interested."

Addie straightened. "She had bedroom eyes for you."

"Still not interested."

"You like having sex."

"True." She'd expected him to go with Chantal. That was why Addie had left. She hadn't been wrong to assume the worst. He'd earned the reputation, but he wanted her to think more of him. "But I'm not some animal who can't control myself. I've been on my best behavior for a while now."

"You don't have to be." She wouldn't meet his gaze. "I mean, we agreed—"

"This is our honeymoon," he said quickly, not wanting to discuss their agreement.

She gave him a come-on look. "Fake honeymoon."

"We got married less than a week ago and we're here together. Sounds like a honeymoon to me."

"Except for us sleeping apart and only kissing on camera."

He attempted a smile. "Gotta start somewhere."

"I suppose."

The humor in her voice gave him hope he hadn't messed up too badly. "You know I'm right."

Her lips curved upward. "I thought wives were the ones who were always right."

"Wouldn't know. This marriage thing is new to me."

She looked up at him. "You're doing pretty well for a newbie. Better than I expected."

Addie's words filled Nick with pride. He didn't want to disappoint her. "Trying my best for my friend."

He hoped that was good enough.

Chapter Seven

I N A PRIVATE, covered structure a short distance from their
bure, Addie sat in the rock-tiled hot tub with Nick. Wind
chimes and white fabric panels hung from the side beams.
Jets sent hot water pulsating against her skin, soothing tight
muscles. An afternoon sea breeze cooled her face.

Another day in paradise.

She ignored Wes and Dylan putting away their gear.
Filming had finished for now. She could relax after an
afternoon of parasailing then floating on a made-for-two
inflatable chaise with Nick while being served refreshments
in the water by resort staff.

Nick leaned his head back. The rocks along the tub edge
had been polished smooth to be more comfortable for guests.
"How many more activities can we pack into these final
three days?"

"Depends on how much footage is needed." She stared at
Nick's profile, his strong jawline, straight nose and long
lashes. So handsome. She thought about what he'd said on

the dock two nights ago. So sweet. The dreamy part of her wished the honeymoon could be real, beyond semantics, but that wasn't going to happen. She looked away, not wanting him to catch her staring. "But unless we slow down, we're going to need a vacation after our honeymoon."

"One without a film crew watching our every move," Nick joked.

"Come on, you're loving every minute of this," Wes said with a grin. "Besides, you can't beat the price of this honeymoon or our wonderful company."

Dylan nodded. "See you lovebirds, tonight."

"The lovo dinner should be an experience," Nick said once the men left.

"Can't wait." Earlier, she'd watched meat and fish be wrapped in banana leaves then buried in the ground to cook. The entire resort had been invited to the traditional meal. Dinner would be served on the beach and a show performed by staff. Dancing to island music would follow. "I'm ready to dance the night away."

"Never knew you were such a party animal."

Oh, yeah. Addie nearly laughed, compared to his wild tendencies she was a couch potato, but she liked to dance when she got the chance. Which hadn't been often except when she was alone and cranked the music. She pushed foamy bubbles his way. "You don't know everything about me."

"True." He raised his head, a big grin on his ace. "But

I'm learning."

Addie could say the same about him. Her shoulder twinged. She rolled her head to the opposite side to stretch out the muscles.

"Shoulder bothering you?" Nick asked.

"A little. Not bad." She rubbed the area. "Must have done something parasailing."

"Let me see." He moved closer. "No bruise."

"Just a twinge."

Nick touched her shoulder. "Hurt?"

"Sore."

"Your muscles are tight." He moved across the hot tub to sit next to her. His thigh pressed against hers. "Sit forward."

She did, then played with the bubbles on the top of the water to distract herself from his nearness and hand on her.

He massaged the sore spot. "How does that feel?"

So good she had to force herself not to collapse against him. If the camera was filming, she would have. Was it too late to call Wes and Dylan back? "Great. Thanks."

"I'm not finished." His expert fingers worked the muscle. "Relax."

Hard to do when she was hyper-aware of everything Nick was doing. She closed her eyes. That counted as relaxing, right?

"Better, but you're not quite there," he said.

Addie couldn't allow herself to go there. Not fully. She might not want to come back. But with each touch of his hands, tension seeped from her shoulder, replaced by a sensual hum. "If you get tired of being a bodyguard, you could make a fortune giving massages."

"Something to consider when I get tired of traveling."

She opened her eyes. "You'll be old and gray by then."

Nick leaned forward, his chest against her back, his chin over her shoulder. He wiggled his fingers in front of Addie. "But I'll still have magic fingers."

"They are magical."

Like him.

"They're yours whenever you need them."

Addie glanced sideways, meeting his gaze, their faces barely an inch apart. Her breath stilled, but her rapid heart rate made up for the lack of oxygen.

Don't get carried away. He was being a good friend.

Friend. Friend. Friend.

"Thanks." She forced herself to move away. Not that she could go far in the hot tub. "I'll have to remember your magic fingers whenever you're in town."

"I won't be gone all the time," Nick insisted, his tone indignant.

"Most of the time," she said for his benefit as well as her own. The honeymoon was almost over. She couldn't give into fantasies and daydreams now. Once they returned to San Diego, things would be different. They wouldn't be together, not like here on the island. She wished that fact didn't bother her as much as it did. But more reason to make the most of the time they had left, even if they ended up exhausted.

THAT NIGHT, TIKI torches lit up the beach. Music played, the beat of a hollowed drum filling the air. Guests danced and mingled on the sand, filmed by Conrad and Wes. Everyone was smiling, enjoying the evening, including Nick.

He sipped his beer, watching Addie dance with two of the entertainers. Her shoulder seemed better, but he would have to be more careful the next time they were in the hot tub. Touching her had felt way too good, and not in a make-your-friend-feel-better sort of way.

But Addie hadn't seemed to mind. She looked carefree, the way he'd hoped to see her since they arrived on the island. The orange flower in her hair matched the floral print on her skirt. Her hips swung back and forth. Her hands imitated the gestures of the other dancers, about half a beat behind. Her feet moved underneath the hem of her skirt, the bottom of her tank top inching up toward the body pack of her microphone. She alternated between dancing and doubled-over laughter.

Beautiful. He would miss seeing this side of her and being together. But the fun couldn't last forever. He would have to be satisfied with the ten days they had here.

Once they were back in San Diego, everything would go back to normal. Normal meant leading separate lives. That was why he knew his marriage plan would work when he'd proposed. His job would keep them apart. The realization unsettled him. He hadn't thought he would enjoy speeding this much time with Addie.

Weird since he and Addie hadn't had a let's-hang-out friendship in years. Visits had been few. They texted, emailed, spoke on the phone, but had made up for lost time on the island.

Addie grinned at him. She flipped her hair behind her right shoulder sending the left side of her hair flying into her face. She shrugged, then laughed. Smooth and seductive, not even close. But adorable with her pink nose. She'd forgotten to apply sunscreen when they'd on the water earlier.

He raised his beer. She gave him the thumbs up sign, then returned her attention to her two dance partners, ignoring Wes and his camera.

Conrad with his red hair filmed Nick. Dylan, the sound guy, ate leftovers. He'd had to fix Addie's microphone while everyone else enjoyed the lovo dinner.

Brad stood next to Nick. "Your bride is having fun out there."

Nick flicked an edge of the beer label with his finger. "Addie loves to dance."

"Why don't you join her?"

Nick knew how to translate Brad-speak. What the guy meant was why don't you go out there and kiss your wife while the cameras are going. "Too full from dinner."

"Not a dancer."

"I dance." Brad acted as if he knew everything about them but Emily had provided the information, not Addie or Nick. "When the time's right."

The music, too. He preferred slow dancing. Only a fool turned down the opportunity to have a feminine body pressed against his and moving together.

"Addie must be used to dancing on her own," Brad said.

Nick's muscles tensed, but he needed to remain cool, play this smart and determine what Brad thought he knew. "What do you mean?"

"Addie mentioned you travel for your job."

Nick's relief was palpable. Brad and crew didn't know anything. "I do."

"Must be hard being away."

"Addie makes coming home easy." A memory formed in his mind. "I—"

"What?"

"Nothing. Something I remembered."

"About Addie?" Brad asked.

Nick nodded.

Brad motioned Conrad to come closer with his camera. "Tell us."

The day seemed like yesterday, not years ago. Nick thought this story would let people see what a special person Addie was.

"After my first deployment, I took leave and flew to San

Diego. Addie and her grandmother, who was in a wheel-chair, were waiting for me at the airport along with a hundred others. She'd asked people to welcome home a soldier while they waited for their loved ones. She passed out balloons, American flags and signs to whoever said yes. I can't imagine how many days she spent making the stuff. Getting out of the airport took forever. Everyone wanted to shake my hand, say thank you, give me a hug." He'd been so touched and full of pride, not to mention affection for Addie. "It was cool."

"A good girlfriend."

"She wasn't. My girlfriend, that is." The words came out disjointed, rough, because the words Addie and girlfriend appealed to him in a way they hadn't in a long time. Old feelings resurfacing, he told himself. "She was a girl and my friend, but we weren't romantically involved."

Like now, he reminded himself.

"The two of you are perfect together," Brad said, to which Nick found himself nodding. "Why weren't you dating back then?"

He knew the reason—their friendship. He'd put that above all else. He still did. "I . . . it wasn't the right time."

"They say timing's everything."

"Addie and I are proof of that." A guy grooved his way toward Addie like she was the lost treasure he'd been search-ing for his entire life. Nick shoved his beer bottle at Brad. "Time to dance with my wife."

He cut in front of the man. Wearing a microphone kept Nick from saying anything, but didn't stop him from shooting a back-off-from-my-woman-or-I'll-hurt-you-bad glare. The guy did an about face and headed toward the bar.

"Didn't expect you to join in." Addie, bright-eyed and flushed cheeks, grinned at Nick. "I thought you didn't dance."

"I dance when the mood strikes."

She arched a brow, then glanced sideways at the camera. "In the mood tonight?"

"Always when I'm with you." Saying the words wasn't much of a stretch.

Addie extended her hand. "Show me what you've got."

As if on cue, the music slowed. Yes, timing was everything, and his was turning out to be perfect. Nick pulled her close, pressing her hips against hers with a possessive hand.

"We're not in high school slow dancing at the prom," she whispered.

"If we were, I couldn't do this." He spun her then lowered her into a dip. He brushed his lips across hers. Short and sweet. Then raised Addie to her feet. "Your date would have gotten angry. Mine, too."

Addie shook her head. "You are too much, Nick Cahill."

"Enough for you. That's what matters." Holding her felt comfortable and natural. He'd never danced like this with Addie. "Our first dance."

"Not quite. We were partners and danced the Virginia

Reel in third grade at an assembly."

"How do you remember that stuff?" he asked, amazed by the memory of hers.

"Well, that was the first time I'd danced with a boy. A big deal when you're an eight-year-old girl."

He winked. "I like the idea of being your first."

She swatted his arm. "You would."

Nick laughed. "Let's see, I was your first fiancé, first dance, first guy friend, first husband."

"Fiancé and dance, yes. But my second guy friend." She glanced at the camera, then back at Nick. "And let's hope my first and only husband."

His breath caught in his throat. He knew she was talking to the camera, but her adoring tone made sucking in oxygen difficult. He cleared his throat. "So who was your first guy friend?"

"Ricky Quintana."

Her hips moved against Nick's while his hand remained at the small of her back. He forced himself not to touch her butt. "Don't remember him."

"Dark hair, brown eyes, carried a soccer ball everywhere, and called people *compadre*."

"Oh, yeah. Chewed lots of bubble gum. Didn't know you were friends."

"He stole things from his parent's gift shop to give me until *you* told everyone we were getting married."

"What else was I going to say? You accepted my marriage

proposal."

"I did," she said. "More than once."

"Second time's the charm."

"I think that's supposed to be the third time?"

"We're in paradise," he said. "We can make our own rules."

"Then let's call it a night and see what rules we can break."

A thrill ran through him, even though this was about ditching the film crew than going back to the room to be alone together.

"Best invitation I've had." He nuzzled against Addie's neck. Man, she smelled good. Her sweet scent intoxicated him. He took another sniff.

She kissed his cheek. The non-sexual peck sent heat rushing through him. With his arm around Addie, he led her off the dance floor.

Brad followed them. "Where are you going?"

"To bed," Addie said without missing a beat. "With my husband."

Pride filled Nick. This was the Addie he remembered, the one who made plans and didn't need anyone to come to her rescue. Though Nick had always been there in case she needed backup. That was what friends did.

Brad's gaze pleaded with him. "It's too early. There's plenty of dancing left."

"We'll be dancing." Nick helped remove her microphone

pack, then handed both to Dylan. "I promise you that."

Brad frowned. "You need to drink from the Kava bowl. Relax."

"I'm plenty relaxed. See you in the morning." Nick gave a wave. "Though not too early. I have a feeling we're going to sleep in."

She ran her fingertip along his jawline. "Who said anything about sleeping tonight?"

If only . . . Nick grinned. "Not me."

"More Kava for us, I guess," Brad mumbled.

Nick didn't turn around. He would much rather look at Addie. The two walked arm and arm along the path lit by lanterns. He hadn't gone ten feet when he heard the sounds of soft footsteps, leaves rustling and breathing. Looked like Brad wasn't admitting defeat so easily.

No worries. Nick leaned in toward Addie, placing his mouth at her ear. "We're not alone. Guessing cameras and a mic at our six."

She sucked in a sharp breath, but didn't glance behind her.

No worries. Like everything else, he had this. "Play along, okay?"

PLAY ALONG. ADDIE would, except the last place she expected to find herself was in Nick's arms, her feet dangling in the air. "You carried me when we arrived. What gives tonight?"

"I carried you over the threshold, but I haven't carried you to bed."

Her heart thudded. *For the cameras.* She repeated the words, but her tongue felt two sizes too big for her mouth.

"If you were walking—" His gaze locked on hers. "—I couldn't do this."

His mouth captured hers with lightning quickness. The touch of his lips sent sparks flying, like tiny firecrackers being set off at once.

Not real.

She tried to focus on what was happening reality TV-wise. The film crew was behind them, following and filming. Nick must know something she didn't because he kept kissing her when she doubted the crew could see anything with lanterns lighting them. Night vision lens?

No matter, she didn't need to know the details. Kissing him was great. She tasted beer, a reminder of Cancun. Oh how she wished he had kissed her then.

The man knew how to kiss. Each time got better. He moved his lips with expert precision, making her nerve endings dance though the only music was the beat of their hearts.

The air temperature had dropped, but her body temperature spiraled into the red zone, her blood simmering, ready to bubble and boil through her veins.

He increased the pressure against her mouth, deepening the kiss. She relished in the feel of him, of his arms holding her body, his lips caressing hers.

A moan escaped. From her or him, she wasn't sure. Nor did she care. All she wanted was more. More kisses. More Nick.

Addie wriggled loose her right arm. She touched the back of his neck, his hair tickling her fingers. One kiss. Two kisses. She lost track.

Muted footsteps gave way to louder ones, but she didn't open her eyes. She wouldn't as long as his lips kept doing what she wanted them to do . . . kiss her.

A floral scent filled the air.

The kisses continued.

She felt herself being lowered, her body no longer pressed against him. Her back hit something soft, the scent of flowers stronger.

Addie opened her eyes. Candles provided a soft lighting, more like a romantic glow. She lay on soft flower petals strewn across the king-sized bed. Mama Lani had set the stage for romance tonight.

Nick kneeled over Addie, keeping his weight off her. He trailed kisses from the corner of her mouth along her jawline, making his way to her ear where he nibbled and kissed.

Sensations shot through her, making her close her eyes and arch up to be closer to him. Her hands tugged at his shirt, wanting to feel his skin against hers.

His breathing matched her own. The only other sound was the rhythmic whirl of the ceiling fan.

The fan.

They were inside. The crew was outside. They didn't need to keep kissing, but did they have to stop?

Nick made his way back to her mouth, showering more kisses. Maybe they could keep going . . .

Lying on rose petals surrounded by candles and awareness humming through her, Addie wanted him. Did she dare? How could she not? She didn't want to live with regret.

"We could make this real, if we wanted to," she said, half-joking, half-serious.

Nick traced her lips with his fingertip. "How real?"

Instinct told her to look away, but she kept her gaze on him. "All the way real."

His eyes widened. "We could." He kissed her lips, then the tip of her nose. "As long as we agree our friendship won't be affected."

She wiggled her toes in anticipation. "Our friendship wouldn't be affected."

"Good to know." He ran his finger along the side of her breast causing her to suck in a breath. "But I thought you wouldn't be into something so casual."

Casual. The word tasted like sand. She was missing something. "We're married."

"Yeah, sort of." He sounded the exact opposite from how he'd described being on a honeymoon. "So this would be spouses with benefits."

Unease trickled through her. She hadn't thought through

want wanting versus having him meant in the long-term. Or in Nick's case, near-term. "So we enjoy each other until it's time to move on?"

"Exactly. We change the agreement for now." He played with her hair. "You game?"

Addie scooted away from him. "I'm sorry for bringing this up, but I . . . can't."

He studied her, an unreadable expression on his face. "I thought you wanted—"

"I do. Or did." She struggled to explain herself without getting emotional. They were friends who were attracted to each other, not head over heels in love. She wanted—needed—love, not a vacation fling. "I wish I could tell you I'm cool with friends or spouses with benefits. That we could spend the next three days being passionate newlyweds, but I'm not some casual hookup you can forget about once we're back in San Diego."

"I'm not going to forget about you."

"You can't. Being your wife complicates the situation." She scooted back. "You're used to keeping things casual with women, but I'm not like that. Things would be different between us. Our agreement would have to change. I'm certain I couldn't handle you going out with other women, even discretely. I'm not wired that way. I'd be hurt."

"I don't want to hurt you, and I'm not into complicated. Let's keep things the way they are."

She nodded, but couldn't quite meet his gaze.

"Hey." He cupped her face so she had to look at him. "You are more important to me than sex. I'm not going to let anything screw up our friendship."

"You're not upset with me."

"I'll need a cold shower, but not upset," he said. "You know I don't do serious relationships. If Carrie hadn't lied about being pregnant, I would have never proposed. You deserve someone better than me, a guy who can give you everything I can't."

What he said gave Addie courage. She lifted her chin. "Can't or won't?"

"Does it matter? I'm the wrong guy for you. We both know it or we'd be having sex right now."

The truth felt like a slap. A part of her still wanted to believe . . .

Don't go there.

He'd said the words himself. He was the wrong guy.

She might want to be a blushing bride to Nick's adoring groom, but there wouldn't be a wedding night. The marriage would remain unconsummated and end in divorce. Fourth of July firework kisses aside, this was no fairy-tale romance. This was a business arrangement. Addie couldn't let herself forget that.

But was this how she wanted to spend the next five years?

Chapter Eight

THE DAYS PASSED in a flurry of activity, swimming and sun, and plenty of fun, but Nick noticed a change in Addie. She sought out Mama Lani, other guests, the film crew, rather than spend time alone with him.

Nick preferred having her to himself, but he understood she wanted space. Better for Addie if they didn't spend every minute together. Once they returned to San Diego, she would be on her own when he left for his new job assignment.

At least he kept telling himself that.

But the truth was more complicated. Carrying her to bed and wanting to have sex had been a mistake. Nick blamed himself, and his actions proved what he'd known his entire life. He wasn't good enough for Addie Sinclair. She deserved more than a roll between the sheets. A good thing she knew she needed a commitment, not casual sex, and hasn't been afraid to tell him.

Dinner turned out to be a quiet affair—crab legs and

fresh vegetables—under a white tent on the beach. Dessert was peanut butter chocolate fondue with fruit, pound cake, and cookie dough to dip. Delicious food, but the conversation seemed forced, adding to the tension in the air. Now back at the *bure*, he felt the same discomfort, as if Addie was trying to distance herself from him further. She sat on the couch, more interested in her cell phone than him.

What happened the night of the lovo dinner had changed things between them, but he'd be damned if he allowed their friendship to continue being affected by his mistake. Time to get things back on track. "Put your phone away and talk to me."

She stared at the screen as if the plastic held the secrets of the universe. "Emily is calling me tonight."

"Her job okay?"

Addie shrugged. "She didn't say. Just mentioned some stuff going on."

"Maybe she met a guy." Nick half-laughed, trying to lighten the atmosphere. "Forget that with her eighty-hour workweeks."

"She'll have a change of heart when she meets Mr. Right." The phone rang. Addie jumped up. "I'm taking this outside to save you from listening to girl talk."

"Okay." Something felt off. Emily had never been one to be in close contact. She was too busy to do anything, but send a text every now and then. He hoped nothing was wrong . . .

SOMETHING WAS WRONG.

The next morning, Nick watched Addie from behind a rock. He couldn't believe he'd resorted to spying on her, but something was going on.

Addie had come in after her call and gone to bed without saying goodnight. Unlike her. This morning she'd woken up early—not normal—and left with Brad, none of the other crew in sight.

One thought kept running through Nick's mind—Carrie.

Okay, he and Addie didn't have a real marriage. But her sneaking around and hiding things bothered him. If she was involved with Brad, she was taking a huge risk given Emily's job was on the line. Nick's, too.

Addie said something to Brad, who drew closer, not seeming to understand the meaning of personal space, at least the American definition. His hand rested on her shoulder. She didn't move, let alone back away.

Not good. Nick's fingertips dug into the rock, scratching the tips.

Brad raised his other arm, bringing his hand toward Addie. She leaned into his chest. He put his arm around her in an embrace.

Nick's muscles hardened like granite. His temperature rose twenty degrees. Addie was his. Brad shouldn't be touching her.

Addie looked up and smiled at Brad.

Nick couldn't watch any longer. He jumped out from the rock. "Isn't this cozy?"

Brad released her, then stepped back.

"What the hell is going on?" The hard edge to Nick's voice sounded strange to his own ears.

Addie shook her head. "Nothing is going on."

Brad raised his hands, palms facing outward. "Not what you think, dude."

Nick raised an eyebrow. "How do you know what I'm thinking?"

"Stop it." The anger in Addie's voice matched the flames in her eyes. "I don't know what's going on, but I'm not Carrie. I've never been anything like her. You said so yourself."

He had. Addie was honest, trustworthy, loyal. Shame burned in his throat. Except . . . "Brad was holding you."

"Offering sympathy. A comfort hug," Brad said. "Not trying to make a move on your wife. I'd be so fired, dude."

Nick's gaze flew to Addie. Her eyes were red, her lashes spiked. He was at her side in an instant. "You've been crying."

"Do you want me to tell him?" Brad asked.

"No, but could I talk to Nick alone."

"Sure. I'll get everything set-up to tape your statement." With that, Brad walked away.

Nick tucked a strand of hair behind her ear. "What is

going on?"

Addie took a deep breath. "Emily saw me on the news. She sent me the clip from the broadcast so I could see for myself."

"Why were you on the news?"

"My aunt accused me of stealing my grandmother's engagement ring and went to the media with the story. Reality TV Honeymoon Bride Steals from Dead Grandma."

"What the . . ." Nick tried to make sense of what he was hearing. "Your grandmother gave you the ring for your birthday. You sold it to pay for her funeral expenses."

"That's what I told my aunt when she asked for the ring months ago, but I guess she didn't believe me. Or maybe she heard about the reality TV show and wants to cash in."

He had proof Addie had sold the ring. Emily knew that, so why hadn't she called him? "I'll fix this in two seconds."

"I need to take care of this."

"But—"

"No."

The force in Addie's voice silenced a reply. He'd never heard her sound so adamant.

"It's time I stand up for myself," she continued.

"Okay."

"It's not okay." She raised her chin, a determination in her eyes he didn't recognize. "I've let my family walk all over me for too long. I need to do something or they'll keep coming after me. Getting the house wasn't enough. Now they want Grammy's engagement. Who knows what they'll want or say I did next? I'm not going to sit back and take their lies any longer."

"I understand. But let me help." Nick reached for her, cupping her face. A touch wasn't enough. He wanted to hold her. "I'm here. You're not in this alone."

"But I was. For the past nine years I was alone."

"I'm sorry."

"Not your fault. Mine." She hung her head for a moment, then straightened. "I could have pursued relationships, difficult as things were. I could have asked for help. I could have taken charge of my future by making sure everything was in order with Grammy's will and finances. But I didn't. I was so wrapped up in the day-to-day activities, so overwhelmed and exhausted, I couldn't think about tomorrow let alone next week. I gave up on living my own life. But no longer."

"You're so brave to do what you did, quitting college to care for your grandmother. You were there when no one else was. That takes guts and strength." He ran the side of his finger along her jawline, wishing he could kiss away her troubles. "You've been there for me the same way. I don't know what I would have done without your emails, letters, and care packages during deployments. You were—are—a lifesaver."

"When you have no life, pouring your emotional support toward someone far away and could use a friend from home is easy to do."

Guilt coated his mouth. He'd never asked how things were going for her, not beyond typical platitudes. "I figured things were tough, but I had no idea they were that bad. I should have known."

"No one knew." She turned her face, shrugging off his touch. "You were off fighting a war and had other things to worry about than me. I never said a word because I didn't want Grammy to overhear me complain. She took me in when I was four. It was my turn. But I should have let people know I needed support. I should have done a lot of things over the years. I can't change the past, but I can do things differently from now on. Standing up for myself against my family is the first step."

"I get it. I do, but—"

"No buts," she interrupted. "I have this figured out."

Her determination filled him with pride. She had gone further than becoming the old Addie again. The new show of strength, of resilience . . . Talk about a turn-on. "Tell me your plan."

"I'm going to tape a statement and address my aunt's accusation. Brad was going over what I would say when I got . . . emotional," she explained. "I want this settled before we return to San Diego. That doesn't give me much time. The producers are sending a film crew to the estate sale jeweler to confirm the ring was purchased then sold to a buyer. They will interview my aunt. The clips will be 'leaked' to the local media and police. And I pray this will be the last time my greedy family drums up phony charges."

"A good plan. Yours?"

"Filming a statement and talking to the jeweler were my ideas. Brad thought of my aunt. He thinks this is great promo opportunity for the reality series."

"Of course, he does. It's great PR and your plan sounds solid." But Nick had her six, an ace in his pocket, well, his overnight bag. "But I don't like Brad touching you."

"He was comforting me."

"I'll reserve judgment."

She sighed. "Brad's not a bad guy. A bit Hollywood, but he thinks the world of you."

Nick rubbed the back of his neck. "I may have overreacted."

"Because of Carrie."

He nodded.

"I would never do what she did to you. Not ever."

"I know that logically, but seeing the two of you together. I wasn't thinking straight."

"Obviously, but I don't get the jealous husband act." She leveled her gaze at him. "We've been having a great time playing make-believe for the camera. But our marriage is fake. You've been adamant about making sure our friendship doesn't change, so why go all green-eyed on Brad?"

"Emotion got the best of me." Not a good answer, but Nick didn't know what else to say.

"If I didn't know better, I'd think you cared about me."

"I do. As a friend," he clarified.

"Well, friend." She emphasized the last word. "Remember our agreement about dating discreetly extends to both of us."

Damn. Nick had been thinking of himself. He didn't like the idea of Addie going out with other guys, but he couldn't expect her to sit at home for the next five years. "I'm sorry for going cavemen on you. I hadn't thought this out. Just acted. I want you to be happy."

"We both deserve to be happy. That's why . . ." She stared at the sand, then looked up, a steely resolve in her eyes. "I can't continue to be part of a fake marriage. I want out."

Air rushed from his lungs. "I don't understand. Things have been going well."

"That's part of the problem." Her gaze softened. "Being with you has shown me I don't want a handsome guy to hang out with and be my meal ticket. I'm not willing to wait five years for more. I want the fairytale, complete with true love and a happily ever after. Now."

Ah, hell. A storybook romance sounded nice, but he knew better than to think that was possible. "I'm not a white-picket-fence, commitment kind of guy. Not sure I ever was."

"I know that." She smiled. Not a forced wearing-my-big-girl-panties, but an I-understand-and-it's-okay smile that proved how special she was. "I used to dream about us being together."

His heart slammed against his chest. "When?"

"High school."

Regret stabbed at him. He longed to go back and do everything over. He swore under his breath.

"Part of me wishes you were still that guy, but you're not," she added, not seeming to realize her words turned his world upside down. "You're happy jetting around the globe and having adventures, and that's okay. I'm not the same girl I was, either.

Addie was worth giving those things up for, except he wasn't capable of giving her the kind of life she wanted. She deserved someone who wanted the same things she did—commitment, family, love. "How long have you felt this way?"

"A couple days, but I wasn't certain until now." She touched his arm. "You're an amazing man, Nick. You've protected me and cared for me, but I want a man who doesn't have to give up what he wants in order to build a life with me. I did that with Grammy. It's not fair. Or fun."

His well-crafted life avoided the things Addie longed for, but standing here, he wasn't sure that was the life he still wanted. Part of him wanted to grab onto Addie and not let go, but he wanted her to be happy. "So what do you want to do?"

"Divorce after the show airs. We can use the pressure of

being on reality TV as the excuse. That way you don't get into trouble with your boss, and Emily doesn't lose her job."

Addie was looking out for others, but she was forgetting she had no money, no job, no place to stay except his place. "I get what you're saying. Being married to someone else will make finding Mr. Right difficult, but where will you live? How will you eat? What will you do?"

"I have no idea, but I'll figure it out."

"What about nursing school?"

"That was my dream when I was in high school. I'm not sure that's the dream after taking care of my grandmother."

"This is so . . ."

"Easy?"

"Civilized," he said. "No screaming and yelling."

"We're friends."

He and Carrie had never been friends. He'd gone home with her the first night they met at a bar. "We've been friends a long time."

Addie nodded. "You're the best."

"Ditto." She was something special. The thought of her giving her heart out to some guy to step on made Nick want to puke. But he couldn't give her the life or be the kind of man she wanted. The urge to kiss her was strong, but he extended his hand instead. "Let's find the crew so you can make your statement and the file can be uploaded today."

She clasped her fingers with his. "We still have to play honeymooners."

"One more day."

Addie stared off at the horizon. "As much of a pain as this has been, I'll miss Starfish Island."

"Me, too." Nick squeezed her hand. But he would miss spending time with Addie like this the most.

AFTER ADDIE FILMED her statement, she sat on the hammock, swinging, nine years of regret lifting away. She'd taken back her life and was moving forward, not stuck in a waiting pattern again. She had Nick's full support. That was all she needed.

So what if she craved his kisses whether the cameras were on or off? Hot kisses didn't make a relationship. Being friends had been and would continue to be their best and only option.

"Great job." Nick sat on the hammock, sending her careening into him. He handed her a water bottle. "I can't wait to see your aunt's clip. She's going to look like greedy inheritance chaser."

"I hope people see the truth." Addie unscrewed the lid, satisfied she'd done what she could. "I want this settled before we get back."

"Nothing like being met by the police when you step off a plane," he teased.

She remembered a story he'd told her about a trip to Florida where things got out of hand. "You would know."

He laughed. "I forgot about that."

"I didn't."

"Obviously."

Looking around, she took a sip of water. The crew milled about on the back patio. Conrad sat on the queen-sized lounge readying his equipment for their next sequence. Dylan sat at the table, listening to something with his headphones on. Wes was filming on the beach.

Brad whistled. The shrill sound sent the birds in the trees replying in unison. "Let's do a quick interview before going horseback riding."

She downed more water. The couple interviews were her favorite part of filming. Brad would ask them a question. She and Nick would answer, playing off what the other said. Easy and fun.

The crew surrounded them. The equipment pointed in her direction was no longer intimidating.

"Where do you want us?" Nick asked.

Brad moved closer. "The hammock is fine."

"I'll say." Nick slid his arm around her. "Cozy."

For now. Soon this would be over. The honeymoon. The filming. Their fake marriage. At least they'd always be friends.

A wide smile settled into place on her face, one she'd perfected with Grammy on bad days. "We'll have to get a hammock to remind of our honeymoon."

"Unless you take home a more permanent reminder,"

Brad said, standing out of the view of the camera, his role as off-stage interviewer.

Her brows drew together. "T-shirts?"

Brad hummed a song, one she recognized, but couldn't place.

A vein throbbed at Nick's jaw. "We just got married. Give us some time before you start talking kids."

Oh, no. Brad was talking about a baby. Her and Nick's baby.

Addie's ovaries' alarm clock blared so loudly she was surprised no one else heard the sound. If she could pick the father of her children, she knew who was top at the list. Better hit the snooze button because without having sex, a baby was not on the horizon. No matter what a beaming Brad might be hoping for, biology was clear on this point.

"But if you go home with a bundle of joy in the oven," Brad pressed.

Nick stared at her stomach. Not totally flat, but no baby bump. That was for sure.

"I'd be thrilled," he said finally.

She knew he was telling the truth. He'd been so excited when Carrie had told him he was going to be a dad. He wanted to be a better father than his had been to him. Addie had no doubt Nick would be.

"Me, too." The two words were all she could manage with visions of a happily ever after running through her head. He was acting for the camera, but the thought of having his baby filled her with a contentment she'd never felt before, and the thought of being a wife and mother with husband and father Nick by her side and in her bed was the most amazing daydream ever. Way better than the ones she'd had in high school.

"That's all you've got to say, Addie?" Brad asked.

She hesitated, trying to compose her thoughts. "I'm sure we'd have a cute baby if *he* took after Nick."

"Or if *she* took after Addie," Nick added.

Fantasy. Not real. For television only.

Except somehow her palm now rested on Nick's thigh. His thumb stroked her side. The temperature had risen ten degrees. Today was going to be a scorcher.

Maybe she should become a teacher. She'd be surrounded by kids at school and get over this unexpected want-to-have-Nick's-baby feeling. Divorcing would help, too. She didn't want to think about this. "Guess we'll have to wait and see, but I wouldn't get your hopes up."

She said the words for the television audience's benefit as well as the film crew's. No one knew this was the least passionate honeymoon that ever happened on Starfish Island. "As Nick said, we're newlyweds. Time together would be nice before we have a family."

"But you've been friends forever," Brad said. "Engaged for what? Twenty-one years?"

She thought back to the little blue-eyed boy with a shy smile who'd helped her when she tripped walking into the kindergarten classroom on the first day of school. If love at first sight existed when you were five, she'd experienced it. Three months later, Nick had proposed to her during recess, right before Christmas break. "Twenty-two."

"Call the *Guinness Book of World Records*," Brad shouted.

Nick didn't say anything.

Addie didn't blame him. She had no doubt he would agree this was awkward. "But we weren't attached at the hip like some kids. Remember when you decided being best friends with a girl wasn't cool?"

"I was what ten or eleven? The teasing from the guys was so bad," he said. "But I was there when your grandfather died."

"I appreciated that. Of course, when we got to high school, you went out with my friends."

"But you were the prettiest one."

"I was the only one you didn't date. Or kiss."

He kissed her forehead, as if to apologize. "You were going off to college and I was joining the army. Why start something when we were going to be apart?"

"We stayed in contact. Though I could have done without the butt dialing in the middle of the night."

He winked. "That only happened . . ."

"A dozen or so times. Less than the drunk calls."

His cheeks reddened. "Shows you who was my last call."

"True." Except, she wasn't always his last call. Not when he was seeing some other woman, however temporary. Their friendship ebbed and flowed like the tides. They'd fallen into a pattern—when one of them needed something, the other was always there. Nick was helping her now. But they hadn't been there for each other day-to-day, and they hadn't taken care of each other at the same time for over sixteen years ago.

Nick raised her hand and pressed his lips against her skin. "Now you're my first kiss of the day and my last."

She kept her smile frozen in place when a part of her wanted to hold him tight and cry for what they would never have together. How many times had she fallen for him only to forget about those feelings in the name of friendship? "And you're mine."

He lowered his mouth to hers. No stage direction needed. They had the kissing down, like the hand holding, intimate touches, and glances.

But this time felt . . . different. Maybe she was imagining things after an emotional morning, but Nick's kiss was more . . . tender.

The way his lips moved over hers made her feel cherished. Warmth flowed through her veins. The heat had nothing to do with the tropical temperatures and everything to do with the man holding her. The kiss was nothing more than another display for the camera, but she wanted to pretend the words he'd said and these kisses were real.

This time she would.

Her left hand splayed his bare back feeling the ridges of his muscles beneath her palm. She touched his hair with her left hand, letting the strands sift through her fingers. He drew her closer, sending the hammock swinging.

Love you.

Addie knew without a doubt she'd fallen in love with Nick once again. As long as he was part of her life, she would keep falling in love with him. Like taking her next breath of air and her heart continuing to beat, she couldn't help herself.

Forget finding Prince Charming. No man would stand a chance against Nick. He wasn't perfect. Far from it, but as long as he and she were friends, her heart would belong to him. Worse, she feared she would find herself waiting for him to return to town to spend time with him. She'd put her life on hold for too long to do that again.

So much for winning the grand prize. She'd lost. Big time.

Shoving aside her feelings so they remained friends wasn't going to work this time. Not after their "honeymoon." And now realizing what she'd been doing these years.

Continuing to be Nick's *friend* would be like living in quicksand, never knowing when she would start sinking, and the descent would be quick and painful.

That left her one choice. One painful, heartbreaking choice.

Addie couldn't afford to keep falling in love with Nick Cahill and pretending she hadn't. She needed to be true to herself, to her feelings, even if she couldn't imagine life with Nick.

But what else could she do?

Nothing else.

She needed to say goodbye. No contact. No anything once they returned to San Diego.

Chapter Nine

AFTER HORSEBACK RIDING, the film crew gathered their gear and headed back to their *bures*. About time. Nick ground his toe into the sand.

He didn't know what was going on with Addie, but she had been the definition of hot and cold this afternoon, kissing him with reckless abandon, which he appreciated, then not saying much, which he hated. He needed to speak with her alone to find out what was going on. "Want to take a walk along the beach?"

"Sure." Addie shook off the sand from their beach towels and placed them in a bag. "A walk will be nice."

Not much enthusiasm in her response. Maybe everything she'd had to deal with today had worn her out. "We don't have to go far if you're tired."

"I'm not." Addie placed her wide-brimmed straw hat on her head. When they were in high school, she was the one who reminded people to put on sunscreen and wear hats when they were at the beach. Might explain why she had such pretty, clear skin and no wrinkles or laugh lines.

Note to self, Nick thought. Make sure Addie laughs more.

She walked along the beach in ankle deep clear water.

He caught up to her in five steps, then shortened his stride to match hers.

She stared off into the horizon, where the water seemed to go on forever. "This place is a slice of heaven on earth."

He laced his fingers with hers. "Paradise."

Addie raised their link hands. "We're not on camera."

"We're honeymooning. You don't want Mama Lani to think we had an argument and want us to have makeup sex." He expected Addie to smile. She didn't. "Worried about what's happening with your aunt?"

"No, I did what I could and I'm good with that."

A middle-aged couple from San Francisco waved from their paddleboards. They'd met the two celebrating their anniversary with a toast at the lovo dinner.

Addie waved back. "You were right about us playing the honeymooners when we're alone. I'd forgotten."

Nick liked holding her hand. Too bad they needed a reason. "I wish we could do this vacation over without the cameras in our faces. I've got an idea. Let's go somewhere for Christmas. Belize or the Caribbean."

She stopped walking, let go of this hand. "Nick . . ."

Her troubled tone made every nerve-ending stand at attention, ready to spring into action. He touched her shoulder, her smooth skin warm beneath his palm, but he also felt a tremble. "Hey, if you want a white Christmas instead of a green one, we can go to the mountains. A place like Montana, one of those luxurious guest ranches with lots of snow and sleigh rides."

Her bottom lip quivered. "I . . . can't."

"Spend Christmas away?"

She shook her head. "I can't keep pretending."

Crap. The anguish in her voice tightened his chest. "Okay, I shouldn't have mentioned Christmas. I know you want a divorce, but I've been thinking. Why rush? You said breaking up after the show was over would be best. I'm leaving on an assignment when we get home. Stay at the townhouse while I'm gone. We'll deal with the marriage when I get back."

The words flew from his mouth, one after the other, a hint of panic, unfamiliar and raw, underlying each one.

"It's not only the fake marriage. It's . . . us."

"Us," he repeated, not understanding. "What about us?"

"I–I . . ."

"Come here." Nick pulled her into his arms in a big bear hug, sending her hat flying. He caught the brim before the straw hit the salt water, then held onto her again, both arms around her. She fit perfectly against him, and he enjoyed the closeness. If only she wasn't so upset. He brushed his lips over her hair. "I'm not sure what's wrong, but it'll be okay."

A sob wracked her body.

"Addie?"

"I love you," she said softly.

"Love you, too."

She pushed away from him. "No, I *love* you. Not as a sister or a friend. As a girlfriend or wife."

Crap. She loved him? Part of him was thrilled, the other shocked.

"I—" He stared at her as if seeing her for the first time. Addie was in love with him? How had that happened? When? "I thought you had more sense than to fall for me."

"Me, too."

"You said you pitied any woman who feel in love with me."

"I do. Just never thought she would be me." Addie took a breath, then another. "But feelings aren't logical. I wish they were."

For years, he'd thought one thing about Addie and now this. "I wasn't expecting this. I need a minute."

Or a few thousand.

Addie wiped her eyes. "I don't expect a compassion-filled soliloquy. Blurting this out and wanting you to say the right words isn't fair to you."

"I'm a guy. You have better odds winning the lottery than me knowing what to say. But I'll give it my best shot."

She shook her head. "You don't have to say a word."

"I want to." He placed the straw hat on her head. "We'll get through this. Trust me. Love is fleeting. Our friendship is the most important thing."

"We can't be friends."

"What?"

"This has happened before. When I was younger. Again in high school. Off and on when you were in the army if I'm being totally honest."

Damn, so much for thinking he knew everything about her. He'd been crazy about Addie, but love?

She inhaled deeply, then blew out the air in a rushed exhale. "I can't keep falling in love with you over and over again. All the kissing and playacting this week has made me face my feelings. I've fallen into a bad pattern. One I need to break. That's why . . ."

"You think we can't be friends," he finished for her.

Addie nodded.

Talk about a load of crap. "You can't be serious about this."

"I need to move on, make a new start, leave the past behind."

"I'm not in your past. I'm right here."

"But these feelings are mired in the past. You don't want a relationship. I do. You're a heartbreaker. You've always been one. I don't want my heart broken."

He touched her shoulder. "I'd never hurt you."

"Not on purpose. But you can't control my feelings."

"Did you ever think you're caught up in the romance of being on our honeymoon? That your feelings aren't real?

That once we leave the island everything will be fine?"

"I know what's real and what's fake. Leaving here isn't going to change how I feel."

His temper spiraled. "So your solution is to go cold turkey."

"Whatever works."

He counted back from one hundred by sevens. No way was he going to turn this into a screaming match and fight. Addie deserved better. "When were you planning to tell me this?"

"Back in San Diego."

San Diego, not home. She didn't consider his place home and never would. The realization hurt.

"But when you started talking about Christmas, I freaked," she added. "I couldn't wait."

Addie had been there for him, most often by text or phone, but there, no matter what. The thought of losing her paralyzed him. "Things don't have to end this way. We can figure something out."

She started to speak, then pressed her lips together. She tried again. "A relationship isn't what you want. I'm not going to settle for anything else."

Not settle for what he was capable of giving her. The thought burned a hole in his gut.

Something told him to fight, not retreat. Except what she said was true. He didn't want those things. He didn't think he wanted those things in the future.

"I know we have to finish filming but please tell them I'm not feeling well. A headache, sinuses maybe. Not the stomach flu. I don't want them to think I'm pregnant."

"I'll think of something." Once the voices in his head stopped shouting not to let her go. He needed to quiet the commotion before he ended up with a bigger headache than he had. "Are you heading back to the room?"

She nodded. "I need a shower."

"Want me to walk you to the *bure*?" The voices screamed at him for asking her, not doing it. "I don't mind," he added.

"I'm fine." Her voice was a quiet as a butterfly. "I'd like time on my own."

"Sure." He hated everything about she'd said. But what was he going to do? Tell her he wanted to be married for real? That would never work. He wasn't good at settling down. He couldn't be what she wanted. If she felt this strongly, giving her anything less would be unfair to Addie, hurt her.

He remembered the times his romantic feelings for her nearly overwhelmed him. When her grandfather died, when he'd thought about taking her on a date, Cancun. He'd pushed the feelings away each time because he hadn't wanted either of them to get hurt. He'd been unsure of her feelings, but truth was, he'd never been sure he was good enough for Addie beyond friendship. He still felt that way no matter the hot kisses they shared. He did know he hadn't been in love with her, and she deserved nothing less. "I'm going for a swim."

She pulled out his towel from her bag.

Nick waved her off. He planned to swim hard and swim far, to clear his head so he could figure out how to fix this. Being wet was the least of his worries. "I don't need a towel."

"Be safe."

The tremor in her voice made him want to hold her until she felt better, but that wasn't what *she* wanted him to do. *He* backed away, moving deeper into the water. "Always."

ADDIE STOOD UNDER the showerhead, wishing the water could wash away her troubles and send them down the drain. Her eyes stung. She couldn't forget the hurt that flashed across Nick's face. There'd been shock, too. He'd had no idea how she felt about him, now or in the past. No one could fake that look.

She'd still done the right thing.

Yes, she'd surprised Nick, hurt him, but she hadn't backed down. Oh, she'd been tempted when he seemed to want to figure things out. But Addie hadn't.

She closed her eyes, leaned her head back and let the water pour down on her face.

Somewhere deep inside she'd found courage. She'd been brave, something she'd forgotten how to be these past nine years, telling Nick the truth about her feelings. She'd been brave, willing to walk away from her safety net—staying with

Nick and letting him provide for her. She'd been brave, and would need to be braver.

No money. No job. Nothing.

She had no idea what she would do when she arrived in San Diego. Emily would be so upset Addie didn't dare ask to sleep on the couch again. But she had the new wardrobe she'd won. A consignment place might be interested in some of the pieces. That would tide her over until she figured things out.

Her gaze focused on the gold band on her ring finger. One more reminder of how Nick's marriage plan had gone oh-so-bad. No one's fault. They thought this would work. Maybe the arrangement would have without the honeymoon and if she hadn't taken a hard look at the person she'd become.

The ring would come off in two days. She hardly remembered the ring was there, but nine days was too short a time to have formed a habit. At least she hoped so.

Her skin resembled raisins. She turned off the water, stepped onto the rug, bypassed the fluffy towel on the rack, and put on her thick, luxurious robe instead. If she concentrated on the mundane, maybe she would forget about her aching heart.

Water dripped from her hair and her body. She didn't care. She went into the bedroom and crawled on top of the bed.

Maybe when she returned to San Diego she would buy a

lottery ticket and hit the six numbers. Her odds of winning the jackpot were better than her chances with Nick. Of course, that would mean her finding a spare dollar somewhere.

Addie stretched out.

No matter how upset she might feel she was doing the right thing. No more putting things on hold or waiting until the right time. She had a life to live. She wanted to live it.

Easy, no.

But she'd taken the first step. She could keep going—right after she gave her heart time to grieve.

TALK ABOUT A bad day . . .

Nick's arms powered through the water with the force of propellers. He kicked like he was trying to get away from the bad guys, the ones who caused him to wake in the middle of the night covered in sweat.

He was trying to escape. Not from memories, but from himself. Addie was correct. Saying goodbye was the only option. He would end up hurting her. The idea he could slayed him. Nick swam faster, accelerating until he reached the shore.

What he was willing to give Addie and what she deserved were in total opposition.

He didn't deal with emotion and romance crap. He hadn't since Carrie, and that had been forced upon him with the pregnancy lie. Keeping things light and casual was the way to go. Having sex was something to be enjoyed, not a reason to call or go out again. But Addie needed more. He couldn't—wouldn't—drag her down to his level.

Nick trudged out of the water, his feet heavy and his breath puffing. He collapsed on the sand.

Ten days on Starfish Island was supposed to be a dream vacation, not the end of a twenty-two year friendship.

The salt water stung his eyes. He rubbed his face.

Addie, sweet Addie. She'd always been there for him. Always loved him. The way he loved . . .

Loved.

What did that mean? How did he love her?

Nick thought about their kisses and carrying her to the *bure* the other night. Playing the role of husband had been easy. He'd enjoyed every moment until today. But he hadn't needed to pretend. He'd been acting this way toward Addie since high school when the guys joked about him being her husband.

Back then he pulled away. He always did that.

Except Addie never let him get too far.

Nick straightened. Hadn't that been the problem when they were younger? He kept turning away because his feelings scared him. He couldn't trust them or know how she would react.

Yes, he loved her.

What happened with Carrie had made him distrust his

emotions more. He hadn't wanted to be rejected and hurt again. Weakness killed. He couldn't be weak. Not for a second.

So he pulled away from anything that might have turned into a real relationship. That should have included Addie, but he could never pull away from her because . . .

He loved her.

She didn't make him weak; she made him strong. He was a better man when he was with her.

Ah, hell. He loved her.

If he ever took a chance at love, the woman would have to be Addie. No way could he succeed at a relationship, at marriage with anyone else.

But would she believe him? Would she give him the opportunity to show that he wanted to take their friendship and phony marriage to the next level?

He slapped the sand. Probably not. She had made up her mind about what he was capable of giving. He didn't blame her. But if he wanted Addie in his life, he needed to show her that he was serious.

Serious, not restless and wanting to roam.

Addie was the best thing in his life. He'd known that since they were in kindergarten. No way was he going to let her go. Not without a fight. He couldn't give up.

He stood and strode toward the *bure*. He needed to convince Addie of his love. Not as his friend, but as a woman, as his wife, whom he wanted to spend the rest of his life with, but how?

All his skills seemed useless. He could drive while firing a gun. He could diffuse a bomb while the timer ticked down. He could move without being seen or heard. But he had no idea how to convince Addie he loved her back.

Nick hadn't a clue what to do first, but someone might. He increased the length of his strides, running now, kicking up the sand behind him. He needed to call Emily. She would know how to help him win the heart of the woman he loved.

And given her job was on the line, she wouldn't dare say no.

NICK HADN'T SLEPT in the *bure*. The next morning, Addie fought her rising panic.

Rays of sunlight brought dawn, but she'd been awake for hours, pacing the length of the room, fueled by a combination of worry and anger. Nick's swim trunks were hanging to dry, and his toiletry kit was gone. He'd returned while she was sleeping for a few minutes at least, but where was he now?

In the *bure* of another woman? Addie's stomach roiled. She didn't want to think the worst of the man, but where else could he be?

"Bula, bula." Mama Lani carried a tray filled with breakfast food. "Time to eat."

Addie combed her fingers through her hair, a nest of

tangles and knots due to falling asleep with wet, uncombed hair. "Thanks, but I'm not hungry."

"You slept through dinner. You need food."

"I need to find Nick."

"Mr. Nick is busy."

"Busy." She gritted her teeth. "Doing what?"

"It's a surprise."

"I don't like surprises."

"You'll like this one."

She doubted that. "Is he . . . alone?"

"No."

The truth hit like an unexpected wave, knocking her flat. Her butt hit the floor with a thud. But her heart hurt more than her bottom.

"Child?" Mama Lani set the tray on the table, then ran to her. "Did you hurt yourself?"

Addie shook her head, not trusting her voice. She was not going to cry. With Mama Lani's help, she stood.

"You are going to sit at the table and eat, then it's time to get ready."

"For what?"

"A surprise filming."

"I can't."

Mischief gleamed in Mama Lani's eyes. "You can, and you will."

Addie would not be fifty percent of a newlywed couple acting lovey-dovey for the camera. Not when she kept imagining Nick with another woman. That strawberry blonde, perhaps? "Please tell me where Nick was last night."

"Mr. Nick thought you needed time alone so he stayed in another *bure* alone."

Relief brought tears. Addie blinked them back. "Oh. Okay."

"Not okay until you eat." Mama Lani led Addie to the table and sat her a chair. "If you don't have breakfast, I'll feed you myself."

All Addie could think about was Nick. He'd been alone. A-L-O-N-E.

Nothing had changed between them, but she felt a million and one times better. She picked up a slice of papaya from the fruit plate. "Okay, I'm eating."

"I'll lay out your clothes."

Addie picked up a *babakau*—a Fiji doughnut. "I'm not feeling well. Nick was supposed to tell Brad I wouldn't be filming today."

"Mr. Nick told me there was a change of plans. He said two ibuprofen should help your headache."

Something was going on or Nick wouldn't have said that to Mama Lani, but what? Addie would do this surprise filming, but as soon as she and Nick finalized divorce plans, she was on the next floatplane off the island.

She took a sip of tea, then wiped her mouth.

A quick sideways glance showed Mama Lani setting out a beautiful white sundress. Addie didn't remember that one hanging in the closet. She took a closer look. "Where did the dress come from?"

"From Brad. Arrived this morning. Very pretty, don't you think?"

"Beautiful." Sundress wasn't the best description of the delightful confection of asymmetric layers of white, a combination of lace and flowing fabric. "But a little fancy for the beach."

Mama Lani shrugged. "Who knows what these television people think?"

"That's true." Addie couldn't believe they thought anyone would watch their show. A happy couple frolicking on the beach wasn't must-see TV. Though female viewers would like seeing a shirtless Nick. "I'm ready to go back to San Diego."

"You leave tomorrow."

"Want to come with me?" she asked.

Mama Lani laughed. "You must return to Starfish Island to see me. I never leave here."

"Never?"

"This is home. My family is here. No reason to go anywhere else."

Addie used to think that way about Coronado when her grandparents had been alive, but she might as well be an orphan after everything her family had pulled. "My friend Emily needs you to take care of her the way you've taken care of me."

"Send her my way. Mama Lani is always here."

"I would if Emily would took time off from her job. She works all the time."

"Too much work is no good.

"I agree." Addie thought about the current state of her bank account and how much a stay on Starfish Island must cost. "Might take me a while, but I'll be back. Someday."

When she took a real honeymoon.

Scratch that. She didn't want memories of Nick to be following her.

"Smile, smile." Mama Lani motioned Addie over. "Time to put on your new dress, then we will work on your hair."

"That might take a while. I went to bed with my hair wet."

"We have an hour."

She stood. "What in the world does the crew have planned today?"

"This is not for the TV crew. There are other things we must do first."

"Okay," Addie said, resigned. "Let's get this over with."

Chapter Ten

THREE HOURS LATER, Nick waited on the beach for Addie to arrive. Hands in his pockets, trying to act calm and cool when his insides trembled, he shifted his weight between his bare feet, the cuffs on his white pants rolled up, sand between his toes. A floral lei hung around his neck, the sweet scent reminding him of Addie.

He hoped this worked.

Thanks to Emily, Mama Lani and the resort's event planner, an impromptu wedding vow renewal ceremony had been put together last night.

Nick wasn't sure about Emily's plan, but after she said his idea sounded like kidnapping and illegal, he decided to go with hers. But he'd added a touch of his own.

A proposal.

Nick would propose. Just he and Addie alone, no cameras in sight. This would give him the opportunity to tell her how he felt and ask her to marry him again only this time for real and on bended knee with an engagement ring.

A simple plan. Easily executed.

He wanted to say failure wasn't an option, but he had zero control on how Addie would respond. All he could do was hope this worked out.

Nick rubbed the ring in his pocket, a lifetime of love against his fingertips. If his words couldn't convince her, maybe the engagement ring would show her how much he cared, not only here but also back in San Diego.

Brad jogged up the beach. His tan had darkened over the past week. His hair had lightened. The guy wasn't as annoying he'd been at the beginning. Nor was he stupid. He'd given Nick and Addie time alone before the ceremony in exchange for a Q&A on camera about why they wanted to renew their vows a week and a half after getting married.

"We're good to go." Brad checked the screen on his tablet. "Ready?"

"Yes." Nick removed his hands from his pockets. The film crew had no idea the true reason behind the wedding vow renewal. They'd been excited by the idea last night and worked hard with the resort staff to set up a ceremony site on the beach this morning. "I'm good to go."

Brad beamed. "Mama Lani is on her way with Addie."

Nick's stomach clenched. "Great."

He'd known fear. Multiple deployments took their toll, but he'd managed, survived. What mattered downrange was his brother on his right and the one on his left, making sure they stayed safe. He'd been part of a team, with the best men he'd ever known, and knew each one would give his life for him, as he would for them.

But here, now, he was on his own. Not a soul to watch his back. Zero cover.

He stared at the water—clear and blue. Gentles waves lapped against the sand, but the rhythm did nothing to soothe his uncertainty, the gnawing fear over how Addie would react to his proposal.

Nick wasn't a pilot, but he'd jumped out of many aircraft. The odds of crashing and burning were high. But he needed to do this. No regrets. He'd have those if he didn't at least try.

"I'm going back to the crew," Brad said. "We'll be watching for you and Addie."

"Before you go. Do me a favor. Stand next to me during the vows."

Brad's brows drew together. "What?"

"Be my best man. I didn't have one the first time around. Though fair warning, you might be called on to make a toast at the reception."

His smile crinkled the corners of his eyes, the first wrinkles Nick had noticed on the guy. "Yes. Hell, I'd be honored. I'll be so on with a best man speech, too. Thanks, dude. Means a lot."

Brad jogged up the beach toward the ceremony site with a spring to his step, leaving Nick to wait.

A few minutes later, plant leaves rustled. Mama Lani's

signal to be ready.

Nick took a deep breath, then another. No game face to put on, but he needed to relax, get rid of the tension bunching his muscles. He should smile, except all he could do was rub his lips together. A silent plea to the friends and teammates he'd lost over the years to take off the Green Beret they wore over their halos and send down some mojo from the bar-that-never-closes in the sky.

Mama Lani appeared on the sand. Addie followed, a vision in white.

Gorgeous. His breath caught in his throat.

The colorful floral garland around her neck matched his. Matching flowers had been woven into her long hair. A beautiful white dress hugged her curves. The hemline fell below the knees, showing off her toned calves and bare feet, complete with hot pink painted toes. She wore no jewelry except a pair of pearl earrings and the gold wedding band on her finger. The ring kept her from looking like a . . . bride.

His heart pounded.

Addie's gaze met his. Something flashed in her eyes. Not anger. More like relief. Her lips parted. "I hear there's a big surprise in store today."

He nodded, unable to tear his gaze away from her. "We only have one more night on the island."

Someone cleared her throat. Mama Lani. Her get-with-the-program chastised Nick. The woman could give an ODA team leader lessons on mission preparation. But one look at

Addie and he'd gotten sidetracked.

"I leave you with Mr. Nick." Mama Lani's tone was loving and nurturing. "He knows what's *supposed* to happen next."

"I do." He reached out and clasped Addie's hand. She stiffened, then relaxed, keeping up the happy couple act in front of Mama Lani.

"See you *both* soon," Mama Lani said. She would walk to the ceremony site from here, using the path not the beach, to be Addie's matron of honor.

But would this wedding vow renewal be for the cameras or for real? Time to find out.

MAMA LANI WALKED off the sand, giving Addie time to admire Nick in his white button-down short-sleeve shirt and pants and allow her annoyance to build. She glanced toward the path. No one was in sight.

She let go of Nick's hand and took two steps back. "You didn't sleep at the *bure* last night. Now there's a surprise when you know I don't want to be part of the filming today. What is going on?"

"You are stunning."

She raised her chin. "Answer my question."

He laughed. "No one's going to step over you again."

"Nope. So . . . ?"

"I've been an idiot."

She wasn't about to disagree, but she had a feeling they were talking about two different things. "What you'd do?"

"It's what I didn't do, but I'm going to make amends." He closed the distance between them and held her hand again.

"I don't understand."

"Let me explain." He took a breath, wet his lips, took another breath. He looked nervous, unlike himself. "Yesterday, you said you loved me. I responded the way I always have when there's romantic feelings between us. I staged a tactical retreat. I thought I could walk away, guard my heart from you, but I realized that's a losing battle. I need to admit defeat. Surrender while I still can."

"You're not making sense."

"I love you, Addie. I always have. Not platonically. Romantically. With my whole heart."

The air whooshed from her lungs. She forced herself to breath. "Stop joking."

"I'm serious. I love you. I was too damn scared of the feelings and how you might react if I told you. After what happened in Fort Bragg, I was plain scared of being hurt and rejected so decided to separate sex and love. Figured I'd be safe. Worked for a while."

"What happened?"

"You. This place. Your honesty about your feelings made me examine my own. I realized how empty my life would be without you."

Her insides tingled. Joy threatened to overflow from her heart. She wanted to believe him, more than anything, but this was Nick. Every word was the opposite of what he'd said yesterday, what he'd said for years.

Addie leaned into him, raised her mouth to his ear to whisper, "Are there cameras on us?"

"No cameras, sweetheart. Only you and me." He kissed her cheek, then raised his hand to his mouth. "But I'm ready to shout the words. I love Adelaide Sinclair Cahill."

"What happened to you not being a one woman guy, not settling down, claiming love is fleeting?"

"Told you I was an idiot."

She gave him a look.

"What happened is I met a cute girl who grew into a beautiful, smart woman. She made me see I was living a lie. And so you know, I'm going to find another job or go into business for myself. I don't want a job that keeps me away from you so much."

A tug of war raged inside her. Was Nick telling the truth? She wasn't sure. "Did you have one too many mimosas for breakfast?"

"I'm not drunk." He raised his hand so she spun under his arm. "Unless I'm tipsy on love."

She laughed at his bad line, then looked around. "Who are you? And what have you done with Nick?"

"I'm right here," he said. "I'm the boy who proposed when we were five. The man who proposed when we were twenty-seven. I'm the husband who wants to propose now."

Nick dropped down on his knee.

Her heart slammed against her chest, beating fiercely in triple time. The scene felt surreal, a dream come true. This couldn't be happening, could it? "Nick?"

"Marry me, Addie. Not in name only. For real. Mrs. Nick Cahill. Nice ring to it, remember?"

The words rushed from his mouth. The hope and affection in his eyes touched her heart. "You're serious."

Her voice was soft, a notch above a whisper.

"Of course, I'm serious. I love you."

He pulled something from his pocket. He held a gold ring between his thumb and index finger and raised his hand. A diamond sparkled in the sunlight.

She took a closer look, gasped, and then covered her mouth with her hands. Tears stung her eyes. "Grammy's engagement ring."

"For you."

"I can't believe this. I was sure I'd never see the ring again. How did you get it?"

"Emily. She told me what you'd done to pay for the funeral. I knew how much the ring meant to you and your grandmother. I roped her into finding it while I was in Dubai."

Addie had no doubt about Nick's sincerity or his love. He'd gone after the ring for her, determined to take care of her when she didn't know he was doing it. She didn't have to worry if his love was true. Like his friendship, his love had always been there. "No wonder she thought we were in love."

"I've been carrying the ring around, wondering when I should give it to you. Emily was confused why you weren't wearing the ring after the ceremony. I told her I was saving the ring as a surprise. Thought the honeymoon might be the right time. So . . . surprise!"

Addie threw herself into his arms, knocking him backwards onto the sand. She landed on top of him. "Nick, oh, Nick. Thank you. I love you. Of course, I'll marry you."

Her lips found his and pressed hard, a kiss full of longing and promise and heat, lots and lots of heat.

"I'm so glad you said yes." He touched her face. "We're going to renew our wedding vows in front of the cameras. We don't have to pretend. This is for real."

"How many surprises do you have in store?"

"You'll have to wait and find out. But we need a proper ceremony this time with a reception afterwards."

She was wearing a white dress. "This is my wedding gown."

"You always said you wanted to get married on the beach."

"I never told you that."

"You told Emily. She did some long distance wedding planning with Mama Lani last night.

So that was what kept him busy. "Unbelievable."

"We should get—Oh, crap."

"What?"

"I dropped the ring. It's gotta be here." He scooted from beneath her and hopped to his knees. "You wouldn't believe what I tracked down in the mountains of Afghanistan. Trust me, I can find a ring in the sand."

Addie trusted him completely. She sat back, her heart full of love for Nick. "I know you will, but I'm going to help."

She searched the sand around them.

He glanced her way, an intense expression on his face. His gazed narrowed on the bodice of her dress. "Found it."

She glanced down. A prong had snagged the fabric on the right side of her breast. "How did the ring end up there?"

A sheepish expression crossed his face. He removed the ring from her dress. "No comment."

Her smile felt wider than her face. She extended her hand. Carefully, he slid the ring onto her finger. A perfect fit.

Addie stared at the ring. "This would make Grammy happy."

"Damn straight. She always thought I was a catch."

"You are, but you're mine now."

"I am." He brushed his lips over hers. "I've always been yours."

She wanted to keep that satisfied smile on his face forever. "Took us long enough to figure this out."

"No worries. We've got one more night left to make the

most of our honeymoon, and we have the rest of our lives together."

Addie stared up at him, her heart full of love. "We won the best prize of all."

"We sure did." Nick embraced her, pulling her against his chest, brushing his lips over her hair. "Each other."

THE BREEZE OFF the cove ruffled the hem of Addie's new white dress. A conch shell trumpeted her arrival on the wedding raft. Drums sounded, echoing the beat of her heart, steady and strong like Nick.

A few minutes later, she stood barefoot on the sand in front of an arch of tropical flowers, the sweet fragrance something she'd never forget about Starfish Island. Her pulse stayed constant, the rhythm as soothing as the waves lapping against the beach, as she and Nick exchanged vows.

Don't lock your knees. Passing out would fuel pregnancy speculation. Not that she was, at least not yet, but who knew what might happen tonight? She wiggled her toes in the sand.

Clicks sounded—photographs being taken by guests and the resort. More pictures to put in their wedding album.

Her excitement built. She glanced at the engagement ring, excitement building. *Breathe.* She needed to breathe.

This. Was. It.

Nick stood next to her. The wind blew the ends of his

wavy light brown hair. A garland of flowers around his neck. So handsome.

Her husband.

Joy overflowed from her heart, rushing through her.

I can't believe this is happening.

Once upon a time, she'd dreamed of marrying Prince Charming. Turned out her schoolgirl crush and in-name-only husband was her Mr. Right. Today she'd been given the opportunity to hear him declare his love, accept his proposal and renew their wedding vows.

Birds flew overhead. The water rolled to shore. Mama Lani stood to her left, dabbing at the corner of her eyes with a tissue. Brad stood to Nick's right, one eye on the ceremony, the other on the film crew taping them. Resort guests and staff filled the white chairs set-up on the beach.

A reception would follow, complete with a first dance on the beach, wedding cake, bouquet toss, and at least one champagne toast. Most likely two. Mama Lani said she might want to make one in addition to Brad's.

Forget the wedding of Addie's dreams being held at the Del in Coronado. All she needed was Nick. The location didn't matter. She thought he was rescuing her by proposing, but his marriage plan and this honeymoon had helped them rescue each other. Everything might not be fairy-tale perfect. Both of them would have to make changes, but they were stronger and smarter then they'd been. Together, they could do anything. No matter what, they had each other's backs.

She couldn't ask for a better beginning to a happily ever after.

"You may kiss your wife."

Nick looked at her, a twinkle in his eyes and a smile on his lips.

This time Addie didn't hesitate. She rose up on her toes and kissed him, hard on the lips.

Mr. and Mrs. Cahill a.k.a. the cutest couple ever.

Those T-shirts would make a great first anniversary gift. A wonderful fiftieth one, too.

Epilogue

Twelve weeks later…

SITTING IN THE posh lobby of the Peabody-Franks advertising agency in San Diego with his film crew, Brad Hammond twirled his pen. Natural light streamed through the atrium ceiling. A pretty, uniformed attendant stood behind a tall counter to direct visitors. The upscale furniture defined corporate success.

Someday…

His cell phone buzzed. He glanced at the screen.

Emily White: *On my way down.*

Brad looked at the three men—his best friends even if they got on his nerves with their antics—sitting in the plush upholstered chairs opposite him. "Emily will be here in a few minutes."

Wes played a game on his cell phone. "Ask her out yet?"

"Thinking about it," Brad said. Although, mixing business with pleasure might not be a smart move.

"I wouldn't. She'll just say no." Conrad stared longingly toward the bank of glass elevators. "But you should see if we can have our meeting in her office upstairs. The views must be amazing."

"Yeah," Dylan agreed. "But they don't want the riffraff messing up those fancy offices."

'They' was a reference to Kendra Peabody, the production company's owner, who treated the business as if it were something to do between her spa days and hair appointments.

But Brad wouldn't let Kendra hold them back. He had no doubt Winning Star Productions would one day occupy a real office complete with a conference room, not the small, two-room space in the basement with a month-to-month rent that he and the film crew could barely squeeze into with all their gear. They were getting closer to relocating. This year, they'd finally turned a profit. Thanks to Emily.

Emily White, an advertising executive at Peabody-Franks who worked for Kendra's husband, Don, had cast Addie and Nick Cahill for the company's reality TV show *Honeymoon in Paradise*. Two shows of eight had run so far. The newlyweds had already captured the hearts of viewers.

This was only the beginning. Brad grinned.

The click of heels sounded against the floor.

He looked over to see Emily walking toward them. She was as smart as she was pretty. A real go-getter. Her short skirt and jacket showed off her curves. A single blond strand had fallen from her updo, but that only softened the hard-nosed business persona she presented.

"Sorry I'm late," Emily said.

Brad and the other three men stood. Each knew they would be out of a job without Emily. She was the brains of the operation, not Kendra.

She sat next to Brad, turned on her tablet, and removed the pen attached to her spiral notebook.

Leave it to Emily to have an old-school method of backing up her notes. The woman was the definition of competence.

Brad hoped her success with the honeymoon show got her the promotion she so desperately wanted.

She readied her pen. "Don's thrilled that Kendra's happy, the sponsors are pleased the ratings from the latest episode were higher than the premiere, and two want to know what your next project will be."

Brad's heart sank. "They don't want another honeymoon show?"

"Not right away."

Bummer.

"We'll just have to come up with something new," Wes said without missing a beat.

Conrad nodded. "Animals are big draws."

"So are supermodels," Dylan added.

None of those ideas called to Brad. He looked at Emily. "Do you have any suggestions?"

Her green eyes sharpened. "Royalty. Look at the popularity of the royal family in Great Britain. You could use a single royal and have him look for a princess bride."

"That's..." Brad tried to find fault in her idea. He couldn't. "Sounds like another winner to me."

Wes nodded. "*The King and I.*"

"How about *The Royal Bachelor?*" Dylan asked.

"I've got it," Conrad said. "*The Search for Cinderella.*"

Everyone nodded.

"But where are we going to find a royal to be on the show?" Brad asked.

"That'll be the hard part," Emily admitted. But ask Kendra. She's one of those society types. She might have connections."

Brad wrote the action item in his notepad. "I'll call her today."

Emily typed on her tablet and then wrote something on the pad. "Don wants to change the name of the company from Winning Star Productions to Ever After Productions."

Don wanted that. Not Kendra. Brad wasn't surprised.

"He thinks that name will lend itself to better marketing opportunities and partnerships," Emily continued. "I agree."

If she was onboard with the name change, Brad would be, too.

"Ever After Productions," he repeated. "I like it."

Wes nodded.

"Me, too," Conrad said.

Dylan made a face. "A too little lovey-dovey for me."

"That's the point." Emily smiled at him.

"If we're going to be focusing on love matches, Ever After is definitely a better fit," Brad said. "Let's just hope we have as good as luck casting the lead as we did with the honeymoon show."

He couldn't wait to give his viewers a show full of fun, royal romance, and a happy ending.

The End

The Ever After Series

Book 1: *The Honeymoon Prize*

Book 2: *The Cinderella Princess*

Book 3: *Christmas at the Castle*

About the Author

USA Today Bestselling author **Melissa McClone** has published over twenty-five novels with Harlequin and been nominated for Romance Writers of America's RITA award. She lives in the Pacific Northwest with her husband, three school-aged children, two spoiled Norwegian Elkhounds and cats who think they rule the house. For more on Melissa's books, visit her website: www.melissamcclone.com

Thank you for reading

The Honeymoon Prize

If you enjoyed this book, you can find more from all our
great authors at TulePublishing.com, or from your favorite
online retailer.

TULE
PUBLISHING

Made in United States
Troutdale, OR
04/13/2024

19166242R00119